...ing author **Rochelle Alers** written more than eighty books and short stories. She has earned numerous honors, including the Zora Neale Hurston Award, the Vivian Stephens Award for excellence in Romance Writing and a Career Achievement Award from *RT Book Reviews*. She is a member of Zeta Phi Beta Sorority, Inc., Iota Theta Zeta Chapter. A full-time writer, she lives in a charming hamlet on Long Island. Rochelle can be contacted through her website, www.rochellealers.org.

TWINS FOR THE SOLDIER

ROCHELLE ALERS

MILLS & BOON

First Published in Great Britain 2019
by Mills & Boon, an imprint of HarperCollins*Publishers*
1 London Bridge Street, London, SE1 9GF

Twins for the Soldier © 2018 Rochelle Alers

ISBN: 978-0-263-27207-9

0119

MIX
Paper from
responsible sources
FSC™ C007454

This book is produced from independently certified FSC™
paper to ensure responsible forest management.

For more information visit: www.harpercollins.co.uk/green

Printed and bound in Spain
by CPI, Barcelona

Chapter One

Leland Wolfe Remington maneuvered off the county road and headed home to Wickham Falls, West Virginia. It had been a long time since he'd thought of The Falls as home. And it was the first time in twelve years that he had returned as a civilian.

Lee doubted whether he would've come back if his sister hadn't called him to reveal that she'd had to close down the family-owned boardinghouse after her live-in boyfriend had swindled her out of her inheritance. Not only was she facing the possibility of the house being seized by the county because of delinquent property taxes, but she was also being sued for large purchases she'd never authorized. The latest love of her life had stolen her identity, and she was facing bankruptcy. It had been on the tip of his tongue to tell her she was too trusting, that she loved with her heart and not her head, but he'd nearly lost his composure as he heard his sister sobbing while she begged him to come back to The Falls to help her reopen the boardinghouse. It was all she had left of their mother's family legacy.

Decelerating, he became a sightseer in a place of which he had good and bad memories. It was the bad ones that had sent him fleeing as soon as he graduated high school, vowing never to come back to live.

His foot hit the brake, and he came to a complete stop when he saw the tall, slender woman walking toward a minivan parked in front of the house where his best friend, Justin Mitchell, had grown up. Galvanized into action, Lee shut off the engine, exited his Jeep Grand Cherokee and waved to the woman shading her eyes with one hand as she held her son's with the other.

"Have I changed that much that you don't recognize me?" he teased as he closed the distance between them.

Angela Banks-Mitchell's jaw dropped. "Lee Remington?"

"In the flesh," he said, smiling.

Lee met the curious eyes of the small boy who was a mirror image of his late father. He had inherited Justin's taupe-brown complexion, light brown eyes and curly hair. Malcolm and his twin sister weren't born when Justin had lost his life while on patrol in Afghanistan. Lee had just graduated US Army Ranger School when Angela sent him a text message about Justin. He had gone to his commanding officer and requested bereavement leave to attend a fallen soldier's funeral, and returned to Wickham Falls to stand in as a pallbearer for his friend. Since that time, he hadn't been back to his hometown—until now.

"There were rumors that you were coming back last year. Apparently, you changed your mind," Angela said.

Angela's mellifluous voice shattered his reverie. Wide-set eyes in a round face the color of whipped mousse held him spellbound. Her delicate features, long legs that seemed to go on forever and waif-thin figure had made her a much-sought-after model even before she graduated high school. Fashion designers were falling over themselves to get her to wear their haute couture, and her agent, who was known to be as unscrupulous as he was skilled in negotiating Angela's meteoric rise as a supermodel, had proved profitable for both of them. She had earned the sobriquet of "America's Naomi Campbell." Lee always felt as if he had lost her twice: once to Justin, and the other time to the glamorous world of high fashion modeling.

The years had been more than kind to Angela. Her face had remained as beautiful as ever, while her body had filled out with womanly curves.

He rested a hand on her shoulder. If the child hadn't been there, Lee would have kissed her cheek. He noted that although her mouth was smiling it wasn't the same with her eyes. There was sadness in the depths of those slanting, dark brown orbs that was a reminder of the loss of her husband and the father of her children.

He wanted to tell Angela he hadn't changed his mind, but that at the time he had been deployed for three months. She waved her left hand and his gaze was drawn to her fingers. Although widowed, she had taken off her rings.

"Believe it now, because I am back." Lee felt a modicum of guilt that he hadn't kept in touch with her following Justin's funeral.

"How long are you staying?" she asked.

Lee dropped his hand. "I'm not sure." His sister had

asked him to come back last spring, but he'd had to decline her request. He wasn't able to tell her he'd been assigned to raids in the Middle East and then subsequently to a war-torn African country.

"One month? Two months?"

Lee stared down at the toes of his military-issued boots before his head popped up. "It's indefinite." He didn't tell her he had given himself a timeline of a year to get the boardinghouse up and running again before reenlisting.

"You left the army?"

He angled his head. Angela had asked him a question he knew would be repeated over and over by those living in The Falls. "I have, for now."

"But—but—I thought you were going to be a lifer," Angela stuttered.

A wry smile twisted Lee's mouth. "Life has a way of changing the best-laid plans," he drawled. The instant the words were out he regretted them. "I'm sorry about that."

Angela shook her head. "There's no need to apologize, Lee. The plans we made when we were teenagers no longer apply."

He nodded. She was right. He, Angela and Justin had written down one wish for what they wanted for their futures the year they'd celebrated their sixteenth birthdays, put the lists in a sealed envelope with the proviso they would open it a day before their high school graduation. Lee had fulfilled his wish to join the military and Angela had had her wish to have a successful modeling career. But it was Justin who had deviated from his goal of becoming a doctor by dropping out of medical school after a year to enlist in the Marines.

His gaze went to the little boy staring up at him. "Hello, buddy."

A slight frown appeared between the child's clear brown eyes. "I'm no buddy. My name is Malcolm."

A wide grin parted Lee's lips. "I guess he told me," he said sotto voce.

Angela stared at her son. Her children were quite outspoken, a trait that annoyed her old-school mother-in-law who believed that children should be seen and not heard. "Malcolm, please say hello to Mr. Lee."

Malcolm blinked slowly. "Hello, Mr. Lee."

Lee hunkered down to Malcolm's height and extended his hand. "It's nice meeting you, Malcolm." The child took his hand.

"Me, too," the child said, as a hint of a smile played at the corners of his mouth.

Angela glanced at Lee. The last time she saw him was at her husband's funeral, and the first thing she'd noticed was his gaunt appearance. When she'd asked him if he had been sick he'd admitted he'd just completed the requirements to become an army ranger, and had lost nearly forty pounds during the extremely intense sixty-one-day combat leadership course. It was apparent he had not only regained the weight but had also developed a lot of muscle, as evidenced by the bulging biceps in the rolled-up sleeves of his fatigues.

Lee was tall, standing six-three, and his striking good looks turned heads whenever he entered a room. The genes he had inherited from his mixed-race African American-and-Cherokee father and white mother had given him a light brown complexion, raven-black wavy hair and blue-gray eyes. The girls at their high school had labeled him tall, dark and dangerous—his good looks, combined with his father's criminal reputation, made him seem particularly lethal in the eyes of their parents, who warned them to stay away from him. *Like father, like son,* she'd heard people say.

But she'd known firsthand that Lee would never dabble in drugs—he'd witnessed how it had nearly destroyed his family. Even when a lot of boys were smoking marijuana, drinking or popping pills, Lee was always an outsider, and she didn't know if it had something to do with his father's drug addiction.

He now stood straight, and her eyes met his as she recalled his question if he'd changed much. At first glance Angela would've said he hadn't. But upon a closer look she saw things that hadn't been apparent during their last encounter. There was a network of fine lines around his eyes, and the stubble on his lean face, with its high cheekbones and sharp features, enhanced his overt masculinity. His hair grazed his jawline, and at the age of thirty, there was no hint of boyishness left in her friend.

"Where's your daughter?" Lee asked.

"Zoe is inside with Lee's mother. Malcolm and I have a dental appointment."

Lee inclined his head. "I'm not going to keep you. Whenever you're free, give me a call so we can catch up."

Angela nodded. There was so much she wanted to tell Lee about the things that had happened since they last saw each other. The year before she'd been hired as the receptionist at a local medical clinic and then promoted to office manager. "Once you're settled in, I'd like you and your sister to come by for Sunday dinner one of these days. I don't know if Vivi told you, but I sold my house and moved in with my mother-in-law a couple of months before the twins were born."

He shook his head and smiled. "No, she didn't. I'm not going anywhere for a while, so I'm really looking forward to getting together."

Angela returned his smile with a bright one of her own. "I'd love to stay and chat, but I have to get going or I'll be late for our appointment." She paused. "I'm glad you're home."

A beat passed before Lee said, "Me, too."

Lee watched as Angela settled Malcolm in a car seat in the second row of the late-model minivan. It may have been years since their last encounter, but time hadn't changed how he felt about his best friend's widow. He'd just celebrated his fifteenth birthday when he first entertained romantic feelings about the girl who told him she loved him like a brother. However, his thoughts about her were anything but brotherly, and he made certain never to cross the line to act on his fantasies. Now, fast-forward more than a decade, Lee realized his feelings for Angela hadn't changed. He still liked her for more than friendship. There were countless times when he cursed his reticence to let her know how he felt, once Justin confessed that he and Angela had slept together two weeks before their high school graduation. And this revelation told him she was lost to him forever. Although they'd promised to stay in touch with one another, he, Justin and Angela took different paths. Lee had immersed himself in all things military. Justin had concentrated on a pre-med curriculum at college, while Angela had taken the world of high fashion modeling by storm.

Their paths did not cross whenever he returned to The Falls for family business. The only contact was an occasional email or instant message with a cursory update as to what was going on in their lives. Lee was shocked when Justin told him he'd dropped out of med school to join the Corps. When he questioned his friend about not following his dream to become a doctor, Justin had said going into medicine had been his mother's wish.

Lee pulled his thoughts back to the present as he clamped his teeth together and watched the taillights of Angela's vehicle turn the corner and disappear. He silently berated himself for not staying more closely connected to the two people who hadn't judged him because he was Emory Remington's boy.

To the men in his unit he was known as Sergeant Remington or "Wolf," but to those in Wickham Falls he was a descendant of the infamous Wolfes who at one time owned most of the coal mines in Johnson County and were notorious for the exploitation of their workers. Although many of the mines had been closed for more than thirty years, Lee could not escape the stigma attached to his family's name. And despite having married a Remington, his mother had continued the family tradition that male descendants who did not carry Wolfe as their surname would have it as a middle name.

Lee exhaled an audible breath. Well, he was back in Wickham Falls, not for a few days or even a week, but close to a year. He would take the time allowed him before reenlisting to rejoin his fellow rangers.

Five minutes later, Lee turned into the driveway leading to The Falls House. For years it had been known as Wolfe Hall, but when it went from being a family residence to a boardinghouse his Aunt Babs changed the name. The century-old structure, designed in the architectural style of the antebellum South, bore noticeable signs of disrepair. Several shutters had come loose from their fastenings, and what had been touted as the finest residence in Johnson County appeared to be an eyesore to Lee. Although the ten-bedroom, twelve-bath mansion was constructed during the Victorian period, Hiram Wolfe's new bride had insisted it resemble her ancestral home in Beaufort, South Carolina.

Lee parked near two carriage houses turned guesthouses that also needed fresh coats of white paint. Repairs weren't at the top of his to-do list, though sitting down with his sister—to ascertain how much money she needed to hold on to the property—was.

Getting out of the car and walking around to the front of the three-story dwelling, Lee rang the doorbell. The keys to the house were in his backpack. He didn't have to wait long for the door to open. The smile parting his lips faded quickly when he saw firsthand the effects of the strain of his sister's current ordeal. There were dark circles under large toffee-colored eyes, and her tawny face was a lot slimmer, almost emaciated, surrounded by a cloud of black curls falling to narrow shoulders.

He extended his arms and wasn't disappointed when she came into his embrace. Lee rested his chin on the top of her head as she cried without making a sound; he massaged her back in a comforting gesture and waited for her to compose herself.

"You came." Viviana sniffled against his chest.

Lee smiled. "I promised you I'd come."

Leaning back, she stared up at him. Looking at his sister brought back memories of when they'd stood outside their mother's bedroom comforting each other after the doctor informed them that Annette Remington had passed away in her sleep. Even though he had been told that his mother was terminally ill, Lee at nine had not understood or believed she wouldn't be there for him and Viviana. The reality of losing one parent was compounded by the absence of his father. Emory Remington had been arrested, convicted and sentenced to five years in jail for the robbery of a convenience store to get the money he needed to pay his drug dealer. Lee would never forget the shame of his father being escorted to his mother's funeral in handcuffs and shackles by US marshals. Although it was a private service, with only family and close friends in attendance, word had still got out that the deceased's husband wasn't permitted to sit with his children, but was sandwiched between two federal police officers at the back of the church.

"I'm so sorry I put you through this," Viviana said, as a new wave of tears filled her eyes.

Reaching into the pocket of his fatigues, Lee took out a handkerchief and dabbed her face. He had promised his mother he would always take care of his younger sister, and he would. "Stop beating yourself up, Vivi. I'll pay the back taxes, and once that's done we'll sit down together and figure out whatever else you have to pay off."

Viviana took the handkerchief and blew her nose. "That scammer stole my identity and ran up thousands of dollars of debt, which has ruined my credit. I barely have enough money to keep the lights on."

Lee stared over his sister's head. Seeing a woman

cry was his Achilles' heel. There were times when he'd snuck into his mother's bedroom to find her in tears. The sight had rendered him motionless when she cried without making a sound. He didn't know if it was because she was in pain, or because she was rapidly facing mortality and knew she wouldn't live long enough to see her children grow to adulthood.

Cradling Viviana's face in his hands, he angled his head. "Haven't I always promised to take care of you?" She nodded and smiled through her tears. "Then I want you to believe me when I say you're not going to lose the house or walk around in the dark. Give me a few days to get acclimated and then we're going to sit together to figure how to get you back on your feet. And even though the house is yours, I'm going to make a few suggestions about not reopening it as a boarding-house again."

Viviana smiled through her tears. "What are you talking about?"

Lee pressed a kiss to her forehead. "No hints. We'll discuss it after we straighten out our financial dilemma."

She blinked slowly. "*Our dilemma,* Lee?" she questioned. "It's not about your or ours, but *my* dilemma. It was me who let some slimeball sweet-talk me to where I trusted him so much that I believed everything that came out of his corrupted mouth until it was too late. I—"

"Enough!" Lee said gently. The single word, although spoken quietly, had the same impact as if he'd shouted. "We're not going to talk about your so-called friend ever again. He's your past and will remain that. I'm back to help you look ahead and rebuild what you feel you've lost. The house is still standing and with a few repairs it will be back in business, good as new."

"That's what I told her."

Lee went completely still when he heard a voice he'd almost forgotten. Turning slowly, he stared at the person he hadn't thought he would ever see again. It had been at least twenty years since he and Emory Remington had come face-to-face, and those encounters were branded in his mind like a tattoo.

Even before and after serving his sentence for armed robbery and finishing his parole, Emory would show up without warning and stay for a week or two. Whenever he came, Viviana was like a kid in a toy shop, laughing with delight that her father was back, but for Lee it was different. They barely exchanged more than a dozen words, and it always was as if he was waiting for the other shoe to drop and he'd wake up to find his father gone. And only when his father left had he allowed himself to relax. It was if Emory had a restless spirit that wouldn't permit him to stay in one place too long. There were so many things he wanted to say to Emory and most of them weren't good, but his upbringing wouldn't permit him to openly verbalize those thoughts.

Emory was only fifty-one, but appeared much older. It wasn't just the snow-white ponytail or the lines around his brown eyes, but the obvious weariness in his nut-brown face that was probably the result of years of drug use coupled with incarceration. What hadn't changed was his slender physique and the ramrod-straight posture of a former marine.

A muscle twitched in Lee's jaw. "What are you doing here?"

Viviana reached for Lee's hand, her fingernails bit-ing into his palm. "Please, Lee, don't start with him. If you want I'll have Daddy move into one of the guest-houses."

Lee glared at his sister. If she had told him Emory was staying with her he would've been more than pre-pared to see the man again. "Don't. It looks as if I'm the intruder here. I'll check in to the Heritage House extended-stay motel off the interstate."

"Lee, please stay," Viviana pleaded.

He forced a smile he didn't feel. "It's okay, Vivi. I need some time alone to get used to civilian life again. Call me when you get all of your paperwork to-gether. Check every place in the house where your ex-boyfriend could've hidden receipts from you."

That said, he turned on his heel and walked out. He returned to his jeep and backed out of the driveway. It took every ounce of self-control not to say all of the things he'd wanted to say to the man who was his fa-ther. For years he'd rehearsed the words he would tell Emory Remington to let him know just how he felt about him. However, time and maturity had changed him to a point where he now rarely thought of the man or how his absence had emotionally scarred him. He had lost his mother, while his father had abandoned his wife, son and daughter.

Lee had discussed his fears and apprehensions with the army psychiatrist, and those sessions had helped him see things in a whole new light. The doctor had pointed out that if his father had been killed in combat the result would've been the same: Emory would not have been there for his wife or his children. It took a number of sessions for him to realize there were dif-ferent forms of loss and abandonment.

As much as he wanted to come home to help his sister, something had him dreading his decision. There were things about his hometown that wouldn't permit him to feel completely comfortable living there again. It had been people with long memories dredging up stories about how immoral the Wolfes had been to their employees, how they'd preferred shutting down the mines and putting people out of work rather than improving safety conditions. Then there was the gossip about his mother breaking her engagement to a boy from a good family to elope with Emory, an aspiring artist, who got a job as a sign maker while he painted in his spare time.

Lee drove onto the county road leading to the interstate. He had wanted to yell at Viviana for not warning him that Emory was back and living with her, but that wouldn't have solved anything. His sister was already emotionally drained, having allowed a man to take advantage of her kindness and generosity, and arguing with her would only acerbate her more about her predicament.

A wry smile twisted Lee's mouth when he thought of how his sister's life had paralleled their mother's. Both had fallen in love with men who had not only disappointed them, but had also broken their hearts.

Chapter Two

Lee parked the jeep in the lot adjacent to the Heritage House. He sat motionless and stared out the windshield as a gamut of emotions washed over him like storm-swept waves. Encountering his father again after nearly twenty years had shocked him to the core, because for a long time the lingering images of shackled prisoner Emory Remington would occasionally surface and prevent him from getting a restful night's sleep.

And seeing him that way had prompted Lee to ask his deceased mother's older sister about his absentee father. Aunt Babs had explained as simply as she could to a nine-year-old about Emory's descent into drug addiction, and told him how his father had been arrested in Tennessee and charged with the robbery of a convenience store to get money to buy drugs.

Even before Emory was incarcerated Lee had become accustomed to not having his father around. The man would come and go every few months, and whenever he asked Emory about his absence, his explanation was always the same: *"I have a job painting a sign and I'll be back as soon as I'm finished."* Lee knew parents had jobs, but he didn't understand why his father's work took him away from home so often.

Lee closed his eyes and shook his head. He was back in The Falls and so was Emory. He didn't know how long Emory planned to stay, but Lee knew he wouldn't be able to live under the same roof as the man because he could not let go of the memories of seeing his mother crying for her husband as she lay dying.

He opened his eyes and exhaled an audible breath. The extended-stay residence, once a motel, had been expanded and renovated. A neon light on an overhead sign indicated there were vacancies. He removed his duffel and backpack from the trunk and pushed open the door to the lobby. The man dozing on a chair behind the front desk sat up when the buzzer rang, indicating someone had come in.

"Welcome, soldier. What can I do for you?"

Lee smiled and noted the name *Leroy* on the badge pinned to the pocket of his chambray shirt. "Good evening. I'd like to check in to one of your one-bedroom suites."

The portly man pulled up a pair of suspenders attached to the waistband of his slacks. "How long do you plan to stay? I'm only asking because we have special rates for folks who stay for at least three months. And because you're military we also offer a fifteen percent discount."

Lee digested this information. *June. July. August.* He would take the three months to settle back into civilian life until he planned his next move. "I'll take it," he told the man with a shaved pate and friendly brown eyes.

"I need a credit card and some government ID." Lee handed him a credit card and his military driver's license. "I have one available with a kitchen that includes a full-size refrigerator, dishwasher, compact washer-dryer, stovetop and microwave. Your suite will also have Wi-Fi, televisions in the living and bedrooms, and housekeeping services. If you need clean sheets and towels, just hang the placard on the door and someone will replenish your supply. I'm only going to charge you for half of June, with the fifteen percent discount of course, and if you're still here in July I'll charge you for that month. We have a policy that you can check out at any time and management will prorate your bill." He paused as he took a copy of Lee's driver's license. "We can't have folks accusing us of cheating them. That would be bad for business."

"You've got that right," Lee said in agreement.

Leroy returned Lee's license and credit card and then gave him two keycards. "Your room is 322. You will find the elevators down the hall on the left. There's an outdoor pool on the other side of the building, and also an exercise room. I don't know if you're familiar with this area, but there are a few chain restaurants and local sports bars less than a quarter of a mile from here. Further up the interstate is a shopping mall. You will find a binder in your room with a listing of stores and shops in the area. There's also a supermarket close by where you can shop for groceries, or you can go online and order what you want and they'll deliver them to you. And by the way—thank you for your service."

Lee wanted to tell the loquacious man that he was more than familiar with the area, but decided to humor him. "It was an honor to serve," he said truthfully. He was anxious to check in to his suite, shower and change out of the fatigues into civvies. Earlier that morning he'd just returned from overseas when he was summoned by his commanding officer and informed that effective immediately he was honorably discharged. Lee had packed up his on-base apartment and then gotten into his vehicle to leave the 75th Ranger Regiment headquartered at Fort Benning, Georgia, for West Virginia.

After changing he planned to go online to order enough groceries to stock the kitchen. His aunt Barbara, whom everyone called Babs, had taught him to cook, and it was something he enjoyed. Even when he returned to base and settled back into his apartment he preferred cooking for himself to eating in the mess hall.

Lee called his aunt whenever he had the chance. He'd grown to love his guardian as much as he had his mother, and when she'd complained about wanting to move to a warmer climate he'd made all the arrangements for her and her husband to relocate to an Arizona golf community where both had become avid golfers.

He opened the door to his suite and walked into the living/dining area. Lee was pleasantly surprised to find that it wasn't filled with the ubiquitous hotel furnishings, but was more in keeping with a personal apartment. Varying shades of green and yellow gave it a tropical look. He dropped his bags and made his way to the bedroom. The vibrant colors were repeated in the wall-to-wall, floor-to-ceiling drapes and the bed dressing. The bedroom was furnished with a king-size bed, a double dresser and bedside tables. There was a spacious sitting area with a love seat and chaise. A desk and chair with outlets nearby doubled as a mini-office. He knew he would enjoy coming here to relax, cook or sleep, while readjusting to life as a civilian for the first time in a dozen years. Lee made his way to the bathroom and peered inside. He had the option of soaking in the garden tub with a Jacuzzi or utilizing the shower stall with an oversize showerhead.

Bending, he untied the laces on his boots and then kicked them off. Within minutes he had undressed and left the clothes in a large wicker basket doubling as a hamper and replaced the lid. Lee returned to where he had left his bags and removed a toiletry kit from the duffel. He lathered his face with shaving cream as he studied his reflection in the mirror over a double sink. His hand stilled when he realized he was looking into the face of a younger Emory. There were times when he couldn't remember what his father looked like because his aunt had removed all photographs of Emory once he was sentenced to prison. It was as if she'd sought to eradicate the memory of the man who'd caused her sister so much emotional pain. Now Lee thought about the times when Aunt Babs stared at him with a perplexed look on her face whenever he stopped by to visit her in Tucson. And he wondered if his startling physical resemblance to her brother-in-law conjured up memories she had buried years before.

Lee knew his aunt loved him and Viviana as if they were her own children, and wondered if she would ever forgive the man who'd deserted her sister, niece and nephew when they'd needed him most. Turning on the hot water, Lee wet the razor and began the task of removing the stubble he'd grown during his last deployment. And like a prisoner counting down the days for his impending release, Lee counted today as his first as a civilian. And he had another three hundred sixty-four before his time would expire for him to reenlist.

Angela sat on a love seat in the enclosed back porch of her mother-in-law's home, watching her son and daughter put together a large-piece puzzle. They'd gone to church earlier that morning, and services were followed by Sunday dinner. Afterwards it was time to relax and wind down before preparing for a two-week vacation for her and a six-week one for her children.

She'd recently celebrated her first year as a working mother. She was employed at a local medical center, and having accrued vacation, she'd decided it was the perfect time to take it. She had never been away from her children since giving birth to them, so it would be a period of adjustment for all of them when visiting her parents and her children's grandparents.

She glanced over at her mother-in-law as Joyce Mitchell concentrated piecing squares for a quilt for her granddaughter's bed. Joyce, a very attractive woman in her midfifties, had been widowed for more than ten years, and had summarily rejected the advances of a number of men who expressed an interest in her. She claimed she was still mourning the loss of her husband and son. Angela hadn't been widowed as long as Joyce, yet she was realistic enough to know Justin was gone and he was never coming back. Every time Justin left on a mission, his parting words to her had always been that if he didn't come back alive, then he didn't want her to spend the rest of her life mourning him. And if she did decide to marry again, to just make certain that the man could love and protect not only her but their children, too.

Joyce had been badgering her to join the military widows' chapter of a local service club, but Angela saw no use in talking to other women about what was, and she didn't want to relive the image of her husband's flag-draped casket before the flag was folded and handed to her. Her sole focus was her son and daughter and their emotional well-being. She hadn't dated and wasn't looking forward to dating until her children were older. After all, she was only thirty and had plenty of years ahead of her to think about having a relationship.

"Lee Remington's back in The Falls."

Joyce's head popped up as she stared over her half-glasses at Angela. Her clear brown eyes grew wider, eyes that were the almost the exact color of her café au lait complexion. "When did he get back?"

"It was a couple of days ago."

"Did you talk to him?" Joyce asked.

Angela nodded. "We chatted for a few minutes before I took Malcolm to the dentist."

"Why didn't you tell me this before?"

A shiver of annoyance snaked its way up Angela's back. Joyce Mitchell was her mother-in-law and her children's grandmother, but Joyce failed to realize she wasn't her keeper. "I didn't think it was important enough to tell you."

Joyce narrowed her eyes. "How long is he staying?"

Angela lifted her shoulders. "I don't know. But he claims he's left the army."

Joyce slowly shook her head. "First we've had to

deal with the father and now the son. What's the world coming to?"

"What's that supposed to mean?" Angela asked.

"Everyone knows that Emory is a convict and a drug addict, and it stands to reason that he could have some influence over that boy, who's had his own brush with the law."

Angela smothered a gasp. "You know that's not true! It was Will Carson who stole Lee's jacket and left it behind when he and his friends broke into the New-man house to put the blame on Lee. And it's a good thing Lee had reported his jacket missing days before or he wouldn't have been able to prove his innocence."

Joyce pressed her lips together until they resembled a slash in her face. "You say that because there was al-ways something going on between you and that boy."

"There was nothing going on between me and Lee except friendship." Angela's voice was barely a whis-per. She didn't like arguing or disagreeing with her mother-in-law while her children were present. But apparently it wasn't the same with Joyce. Whatever she thought came out of her mouth without being cen-sored first.

Joyce snorted under her breath. "He didn't think I noticed, but there were times when he couldn't take his eyes off you."

Angela bit her lip to keep from screaming at the older woman. "Lee was and is my friend and that's all he'll ever be to me. And you're wrong about Lee liking me beyond friendship."

Joyce placed her quilting in the basket next to her chair. "Are you saying you'll be seeing him again?"

"Yes, and for as long as he's here. I've never judged

Lee for what his father did years ago. The man paid his debt to society and it's only narrow-minded people who are not willing to forgive and forget."

Joyce sat straight. "Are you saying I'm narrow-minded?"

Angela wanted to tell her she was, but knew it would start something that would escalate into a full-blown spat resulting in hurt feelings. "All I'm saying is that if Lee reaches out to me, then I'm not going to reject him. I was going to invite him and his sister over for Sunday dinner but judging how you feel about him that's not going to happen."

"I just don't want him around my grandson because you know Malcolm's been asking about finding a daddy."

Counting slowly to ten so she wouldn't say something that would completely fracture her relationship with Malcolm and Zoe's grandmother, Angela took deep breaths. "You seem to forget that your grandson and daughter are *my* children and as such I decide where they live and who they see. You raised your son, and now please let me raise mine."

Much to Angela's surprise, Joyce's eyes filled with tears, and suddenly she felt remorse for speaking so harshly. But they had reached a point in their relationship when Joyce sought to control her life and those of her children as she'd done with Justin, who'd sometimes joked that his father died just to get away from his mother's constant nagging. That no one could make Joyce happy even if they gave her everything she'd ever wanted. And it wasn't for the first time that Angela blamed herself for selling the house her parents had given her and Justin as a wedding gift, after they moved to Florida to teach at a historically black university.

Two months before she was scheduled to give birth she'd put the house where she'd grown up with her brother on the market to move in with Joyce. Now, in hindsight, she realized it was an action based on impulse and not common sense. It wasn't that she hadn't been more than aware of Justin's mother's controlling personality, but at that time she'd been vulnerable and had allowed the woman to make all her decisions for her.

Grieving the loss of her husband and giving birth to twins had proved overwhelming for a first-time mother. Her mother had taken family leave to come up and stay with her for a month, and after witnessing Joyce's domineering behavior she'd invited Angela to move to Florida. Even her brother had urged her to relocate to the West Coast to be close to his family, but Angela did not want to leave Wickham Falls because her husband was buried there.

Reaching for a tissue in a box near a side table, Joyce dabbed her eyes. "I know I can get a little pushy, but my grandkids are all I have left to remind me of my son."

Angela felt a pang of guilt that she had to be reminded of Joyce's loss. Not only had Joyce lost her husband but also her only child. "I know that. But you should realize Malcolm isn't Justin, and no matter how much you try to mold him into his father's image he is his own little person."

Joyce sniffled softly. "I'm sorry, Angela, if you think I'm trying to raise your children. No one knows better than me that you're a very good mother, and I'm honored to call you daughter. I suppose I'm overreacting, anticipating not seeing the kids for the summer when they go to Florida to stay with your folks."

Rising from the love seat, Angela leaned over and kissed Joyce's short salt-and-pepper curls. "I'm going upstairs to finish packing. After that I'll be down to give the kids their bath."

A smile parted the older woman's lips. "Okay."

Angela walked off the porch and made her way up the staircase to the second story. She entered her bedroom and closed the door behind her. Flopping down on a cushioned rocker, she pulled her lip between her teeth. It was getting more and more difficult to live under the same roof as her children's paternal grandmother, whom they adored. There were occasions when she contemplated contacting the local real estate agent to look for a house in The Falls.

Angela picked up her cell phone and scrolled through her directory until she found Lee's name. She needed to talk to him if only to stop thinking about what was becoming an escalating situation with her mother-in-law. And he had always been the one she had gone to whenever she and Justin occasionally broke up for weeks, before reconciling as if nothing had happened.

He picked up after two rings. "What's up, Angie?" She smiled when she heard his warm greeting.

"I hope you've settled in The Falls House okay."

There was a pause before he said, "I'm not staying at The Falls House. I've checked in to the Heritage House extended stay off exit 15."

A slight frown appeared between her eyes. "Why?"

There came another pause. "I'll explain it when I see you in person."

"You won't see me for the next two weeks."

"Why?"

"I'm taking the twins down to Daytona Beach to stay with my folks for the summer. I've decided to spend two weeks with them. I should be back by July 2."

"How are your parents?"

"They're well. This is the first summer they're going to spend time with their youngest grandchildren."

"What about your brother's kids?"

Angela kicked off her sandals and rested her feet on a cushioned footstool. "They're enrolled in a tennis camp for the summer."

"How old are they now?"

"Kendra's ten and Mariah's eight."

Lee's chuckle came through the earpiece. "Talk about the second coming of Venus and Serena Williams."

It was Angela's turn to laugh. "Now you sound like my brother."

"Are they good, Angie?"

She nodded. "Yes. In fact, they're very good."

"Well, it looks as if everyone's doing well."

Angela closed her eyes. "Not everyone."

"What's the matter?"

She heard the concern in Lee's voice, and decided to be truthful. "I'm not getting along with Justin's mother."

"What's going on?" Lee asked.

Angela opened her eyes and stared at a photograph of her and Justin, taken right before he was deployed. She'd just discovered she was pregnant, but was unaware that she was carrying two babies. "She can't stop meddling in my life. Now that I look back I realize selling my house and moving in with her was one of the worst decisions I've ever made."

"Is it meddling or concern?"

"Why are you taking her side?"

"I'm not taking sides, Angela. After all, you're a widow with two young children, and maybe she's just being overprotective."

"Please don't get me wrong, Lee. I appreciate all she's done for me, but I'd like to be able to raise my children without her telling me what I should or shouldn't do with them."

"Have you thought of getting your own place?"

She smiled. "Lately I have. Even though my parents have been nagging me to move to Florida and buy a house in their gated community, I don't want to leave The Falls because Justin's buried here."

"If you don't want to leave The Falls, you should be able to find a house to fit your needs or lifestyle."

Angela's smile grew wider. Lee had just echoed her notion about buying a house in her hometown. "You're probably right. Once I come back I'm going to contact a real estate agent and see if she has any listings within my price range." She wasn't a pauper, and neither was she wealthy. She'd saved most of her earnings from modeling, given half the proceeds from the sale of her parents' house to them for their future retirement, and invested Justin's military combat death benefit in a college fund for her children.

"When are you leaving for Florida?" Lee asked.

"Tomorrow morning."

"Are you flying or driving?"

"I'm driving. Barring delays it should take about ten hours."

"Drive carefully."

"I will. And thanks, Lee."

"What are you thanking me for?"

A hint of a smile touched the corners of her mouth. "For letting me bare my soul."

"Don't even go there, Angela. How many times have you listened to me go on about what was going on my life and what I wanted for my future? And it was the same with Justin. Remember when we put our wish lists in that sealed envelope with a promise we would open it the day before graduation?"

"How can I forget?"

"It was also the day we promised each other that we were friends for life, and that we would always be there for one another. And that means in the good and bad times, Angela. So, you don't ever have to thank me for anything."

"I want to thank you one last time for reminding me of that. I'm going to hang up now because I have to finish packing. I'll be in touch once I get back."

"I'll be here."

Angela couldn't help smiling. She placed the phone on the bedside table and thought about what Joyce had said about Leland liking her beyond friendship. He'd always treated her with respect and told her if she ever needed him for anything he would be there for her. And if he did love her, then it was not as a boyfriend, but like a sister.

Angela walked over to the closet to select what she needed to pack for her vacation. It was the first time in more than a year that she would take a break from the medical office where she had initially been hired as a receptionist.

She hadn't planned to reenter the workforce until her children were enrolled in school, but when she heard that Dr. Henry Franklin was looking for someone to work the front desk after his longtime employee relocated to Delaware to care for her elderly father, Angela had submitted her application and had been hired despite not having any prior office experience. She'd taken to her position like a duck to water, and had been promoted to office manager soon after because of her organizational skills. Dr. Franklin had also taken on a partner, Dr. Natalia Hawkins, and the result was that the wait time to treat patients was cut in half.

Working outside the home offered Angela the opportunity to vary her daily routine. The first week she'd experienced guilt at leaving her son and daughter and made it a point to come home during her lunch break to be with them. At first they were glad to see her, chatting excitedly about what they had done with Grammie, but Joyce had changed their schedule and Angela had found them napping whenever she arrived.

It had taken a while, and Angela didn't want to believe she was suspicious or even paranoid, but she couldn't shake the notion that her mother-in-law was using subtle methods to drive a wedge between her and Malcolm and Zoe. And it was Malcolm in particular. Not only did he look like Justin, he was also bright for his age—articulate, curious and outgoing—while Zoe was shy and more reserved.

She thought about the terse back-and-forth with Joyce about Lee. Joyce's views about her friend and his father were echoed and believed by so many in The Falls that it was difficult to find someone who thought otherwise. However, Angela was different. She'd liked Lee from the moment she and Justin befriended him in the high school cafeteria. She'd seen him around town, and was as surprised as a lot of kids when he had transferred from a private Catholic institution to the local high school. Angela found him more mature than most boys their age, and despite living in what most called a mansion he was modest and unpretentious.

Did she like him? Yes. Was she in love with him? No. Justin Mitchell was the love of her life, the only man she'd slept with, and she doubted if she would ever fall in love again.

Angela piled slacks, blouses and several sundresses on a chair before taking out a Pullman, and then made quick work of packing her clothes.

Chapter Three

Lee opened the door to his sister's knock. The first thing he noticed was that she didn't look as tired as she had the week before. Pulling her into the suite, he dropped a kiss on her hair. She had blown out the curls and in its place was a cascade of raven strands sweeping down her back.

"Welcome to my humble abode."

Viviana smiled and the gesture lit up her brown eyes. "It doesn't look that humble to me. I've passed this place a number of times and never knew it looked like this inside."

"I was also quite surprised," Lee admitted. He had spent the past few days catching up on sleep, swimming laps in the outdoor pool, working out in the exercise room and binge-watching a favorite TV series of which he'd missed a few episodes. The suite had everything he'd want if he was looking to rent a furnished apartment. "How are you?"

"Much better now that you're here." She sniffed the air. "Something smells good."

Reaching for her hand, Lee eased the canvas tote from her fingers and placed it on a side table. He led her into the dining area and pulled out a chair to seat her at the table set for two. "I decided we'd eat before wading through what I expect is tons of paper."

Viviana's expression sobered. "And it's more paper and receipts than I'd expected to find. I still can't believe that rat hid bills that the mail carrier delivered to the house. And it wasn't until the bank manager called and told me that I'd overdrawn my line of credit that I realized something was wrong."

"We'll talk about your rat later, but right now I need you to tell me how much you need to cover the delinquent property taxes." Lee schooled his expression not to reveal his shock when Viviana quoted a figure that was a lot more than he'd anticipated. "That can't be for one year."

"It's for two years."

"I'll make arrangements to get a bank check and then drive over to the county offices and take care of it."

Viviana lowered her eyes. "I'm sorry you have to dip into your savings to bail me out. As soon as the boardinghouse is up and running again I promise to pay you back."

Lee smiled. "Did I say anything about you paying me back? Remember, I own half the property, so I do have a personal stake in keeping it in the family."

Their mother's will bequeathed them the house and

the twelve acres on which it sat. He and Viviana were also equal recipients of their mother's life insurance. The terms of the policy had designated her older sister Barbara Wolfe-McCarthy as executor and legal guardian for her children until they were eighteen. Lee had taken control of his trust months before enlisting in the army, purchasing ten-year tax-free municipal bonds. Once they matured he'd reinvested half in a retirement fund and purchased certificates of deposits with the remaining half, while Vivi had used her inheritance to pay for college and set up a partnership with their aunt and uncle to convert The Falls House from a private residence to a boardinghouse.

"I can't believe I trusted someone so much that I wasn't able to see what was right in front of me. His online profile was almost picture-perfect. I'm definitely through with online dating sites."

"I didn't invite you here for a pity party, Vivi. What's done is done, and hopefully it will never happen again."

Viviana met her brother's large eyes, eyes that reminded her of their mother's. When he'd walked into The Falls House, she was seeing him for the first time in nearly four years, and she was shocked at how much he resembled their father. He could have been Emory Remington's younger clone, except for the eye color. She was only two years younger than Lee, but there were times when she felt he was more of a father figure to her than an older brother. She was also aware that if he did come back to Wickham Falls it would be to visit, but never to live again.

Days before he was scheduled to leave for basic training he'd told Viviana there were too many bad memories to make him feel at home in his place of birth. However, he did come back to attend her high school and college graduations, and to sign the legal documents transferring half their share of the boardinghouse to Aunt Babs before she relocated to Arizona. He had also come back for the funeral of Justin Mitchell. Not only had he looked different, but something inwardly had changed. There was a vacant look in his eyes that frightened her, and he didn't speak unless spoken to. He'd stayed long enough to pay his respects, and then he was gone.

"What are you making?" she asked, changing the topic of conversation.

"Your favorite: rack of lamb with mint sauce, roasted asparagus and rosemary potato wedges."

Viviana smiled. "You remembered."

Lee opened the oven to check on the meat. "There aren't too many things I forget."

"Like Dad being gone more than he was here?"

He went completely still. "I really don't want to talk about him now."

"Sorry about that."

"There's no need to apologize, Vivi. I'm just not ready to relive the past."

She nodded. He didn't want to talk about the past and she did. Times had changed and so had their father, so she decided to bide her time before broaching the subject again. Pushing back the chair, Viviana rose to her feet and walked over and stood next to Lee as he blended fresh mint leaves, confectioners' sugar and cider vinegar in a mini food processor.

"Have you thought about getting married?"

"No. Why would you ask me that?"

"I just thought you would've been married and made me an aunt by the time you were thirty."

He gave her a sidelong smile. "I could say the same about you making me an uncle."

Viviana affected a frown. "Not with my track record for attracting lowlife vermin masquerading as the opposite sex."

"Maybe men see you as an easy mark because you smile and talk to everyone."

"Well, I do have a background in advertising, marketing and hotel hospitality."

"You have to separate the business hospitality from the personal one. What works when greeting guests and working the front desk shouldn't carry over to becoming personally involved with a man."

She paused. "I don't know what it is, but I go on a hiatus where I won't date anyone for months or even a year, and then when I do he's usually not worth wasting my time with."

Lee wiped his hands on a terry cloth towel after blending the ingredients in the food processor and spooned it into a small glass bowl. "Don't beat yourself up, Vivi. Men go through the same thing. I've met women who I feel may be that special one, and then without warning she'll change into someone I don't recognize."

"Do you think it's difficult for you to form a lasting relationship with a woman because you don't know when you're going to be deployed?"

"That and a few other things."

Resting her hip against the countertop, Viviana stared at her brother. "Do the few other things include you thinking you'll not be a good husband or father?"

She froze when Lee impaled her with a lethal stare that sent chills up and down her body despite the heat coming from the oven.

"I saw firsthand how *not* to take care of my wife and children."

Viviana's eyelids fluttered. She didn't know what all had gone on between her parents, because most times Aunt Babs had made excuses about her father's frequent absences and had attempted to shield her from the disease that changed her mother from a happy young woman into one who spent more time sleeping than awake. Even when Lee elected to attend the local high school, she'd continued her classes at the parochial boarding school because she didn't want to leave her friends. And that meant coming home during school recess and holidays and occasionally some weekends.

"Is there anything I can help you with? I feel so helpless standing around watching you cook." Aunt Babs had taught her and Lee to cook. Her aunt had graduated culinary school but her career was short-circuited when Babs returned to The Falls House to care for her sister, niece and nephew.

"I didn't know if you want wine with your meal, but just in case I bought a couple of bottles of white, rosé and red."

Lee's voice broke into her thoughts. "I'll have rosé but only if you'll join me." Viviana knew Lee rarely drank, and if he did it was either a glass of wine or beer, but never hard liquor.

"The wine is in the fridge, and the corkscrew is in the drawer on your right."

Twenty minutes later Viviana sat down with Lee to enjoy the most delicious meal she had had in months.

Once she'd discovered her ex's duplicity she was unable to eat more than a few morsels before feeling full. She exhaled an audible sigh after swallowing a tender slice of lamb. Her world had righted itself. Her brother was back and so was her father, the latter informing her he was only going to spend a few weeks in The Falls before returning to Philadelphia—a city that was now his permanent home.

Over dinner they discussed Lee's proposal to turn The Falls House into a bed-and-breakfast, while both agreed that she should file for chapter 7, which would wipe out her debt, allow her to keep her assets, rebuild her credit, incorporate another business, make repairs and start anew. His next suggestion rendered her mute for a full minute.

"You want to sell off more land?" she asked, once she recovered her voice.

Lee laced his fingers together. "Not all of it. Every generation since the turn of the twentieth century sold large parcels of the original two hundred thirty acres. The house and outbuildings sit on twelve acres. If we sell eight, then you'll have more than enough money to make repairs and put some away for your retirement."

She blinked slowly. "But the land is a part of our legacy."

"What legacy, Vivi? We are the last of the Wolfes and the exterior of the house is falling apart. I've told you that I'm going to stay long enough and help you get your business up and running and then I'm out of here. So if you want to hold on to the property, then you cannot continue to go down the same path."

Viviana knew Lee was right. What once had been the grandest house in Johnson County was now becoming a shabby replica of what it had been. "I'll think about it," she said, not willing to give in that easily to her brother's proposal to sell off the land that had been in their family for more than a century.

"Don't think too long," Lee said softly.

She ran her fingers through her hair and closed her eyes. So much had happened over the past year to turn her life into a nightmare. Creditors were calling incessantly, asking for money she didn't have, and three months ago, she had given employees and lodgers of the boardinghouse notice that she was going out of business. Viviana opened her eyes and gave Lee a long, penetrating stare.

"It is a lot to think about."

A hint of a smile played at the corners of his mouth. "I know it is, but gone are the days when the Wolfes had an active social calendar when they entertained friends and elected officials. And even if you do decide to marry and start a family I doubt if you'll have enough children to fill ten bedroom suites like our relatives did in the past."

"I doubt if I'll ever marry and have children."

Lee winked at her. "Don't say *ever*, little sister."

"Enough talk about marriage and babies. Do you want me to call Preston McAvoy's office and set up a meeting to discuss filing for bankruptcy and setting up a new corporation?" she asked.

"Yes, and try and come up with several names for the new business. Meanwhile, I'll cover the past-due taxes and utilities."

Viviana pulled her lip between her teeth for several seconds. "Dad paid the electric bill."

Lee sat straight. "I don't want you to accept any more money from him."

Viviana knew Lee didn't want to talk about their father, but she did. When Emory offered to pay the delinquent electric bill she'd wanted to tell him that he was twenty years too late in his attempt to play the supportive father, but had held her tongue. Even if he hadn't been able to provide for his family financially, she'd realized once she was older that he could have been there emotionally for them.

"I didn't ask him. He volunteered." She didn't want to argue with Lee about their father. And she didn't want Emory involved in something that had nothing to do with him. His name did not appear on any of the documents in connection with the main house, the guesthouses or the land. "I'll make certain not to involve him again."

Lee gave her a barely perceptible nod. "Thanks. You have a lot on your plate before the B and B is up and running, and that means prioritizing."

"You're right. I think we should take care of legal matters first." Reaching for a pencil and pad she began jotting down possible names for the new corporation. Her hand stilled. "I did something I never thought I would do."

"What's that?" Lee asked, as he stood up and began clearing the table.

"I posted a photo of Marcus on a number of social media sites with a warning that he's an identity thief. Hopefully someone will recognize him and call the authorities."

Lee's eyebrows lifted slightly. "Scamming you probably wasn't his first rodeo, and if he's done this before then someone is sure to recognize him."

Viviana pushed back her chair, stacked plates and flatware, and joined Lee in the kitchen. "That's what I'm hoping." She pressed her lips together when she recalled meeting Marcus for the first time. He was everything she wanted in a man, and then some, but that was before she realized he'd hustled her. "You're probably right about that. Everything about him was so calculating and I…" Her words trailed off when Lee's cell phone rang.

Wiping his hands on a towel, Lee picked up the phone and glanced at the display. "I have to take this." Angela was calling him again. He tapped a button. "How's it going?"

"Great. I just called to say I'm back in The Falls."

Lee turned his back when he noticed Viviana staring at him. "I thought you were going to be away for two weeks," he said under his breath.

"That was before my parents decided to fly to LA and take Malcolm and Zoe with them. My kids were beside themselves once they discovered they were going on a plane for the first time."

"Can I call you back later, because I'm having dinner with my sister?"

"No problem. Call me whenever you get the chance."

He smiled. "I will."

"Who was she?" Viviana asked once he ended the call.

He set the phone on the countertop. "What are you talking about?"

"I know you were talking to a woman because your voice changed. Have you been holding out on me?"

"No. And for your information, Miss Busybody, the woman is Angela."

"Angela Banks?"

"Remember she's now Angela Mitchell."

Viviana snorted under her breath. "It appears as if you haven't wasted any time hooking up with your best friend's widow."

A frown appeared between his eyes. "What's that supposed to mean?"

"I always thought Angela married the wrong friend."

"You don't know what you're talking about, so get your mind out of the gutter because I have no intention of *hooking up* with her."

Viviana held up her hands. "Don't get me wrong, Lee. I happen to like Angela and wouldn't mind having her as a sister-in-law and becoming an auntie to her adorable twins."

Lee smiled when he should've told Viviana to stop meddling in his life. "I never figured you for a matchmaker."

"That's because I'm a true romantic at heart."

He tugged on the end of her unbound hair. "Let me know when you're ready to meet a nice guy and I'll introduce you to one of my buddies."

Viviana scrunched up her pert nose. "Nice, or even close to perfect, but no thanks. I need to concentrate on reviving the business before I even consider looking at another man."

Lee dropped a kiss on his sister's hair. "It's going to happen, and when you reopen it will be better than before."

Wrapping her arms around Lee's waist, Viviana rested her head against his shoulder. "That's what I always like about you. You're always so optimistic."

He wanted to tell her that optimism was what allowed him to survive dangerous missions. And whenever Lee went out with his team his sole focus was completing what he'd been ordered to accomplish and return alive. "Why don't you go home before it gets too dark."

She lowered her arms. "Don't you want me to help you clean up?"

"No. Everything can go into the dishwasher."

Viviana kissed Lee's cheek and then gathered her tote as he walked her to the door. She smiled up at him. "You're the best brother a sister could ever have."

He winked at her. "That goes double for me when it comes to choosing a sister. Text and let me know when you get an appointment with the lawyer."

"I will."

Lee closed and locked the door behind her, and then returned to the kitchen to finish loading the dishwasher. On average, he and Viviana communicated several times a month, either Skyping or through text messages. He'd felt obligated to let her know that he was all right, because aside from their Aunt Babs he was her only other surviving relative. And they'd agreed to give each other power of attorney for all legal matters if he wasn't available to sign in person. There were few things they hid from each other—the exception was his missions—and what he found odd was her not mentioning that her relationship with her latest boyfriend had ended nearly four months earlier. It was only when she received a notification that the property would be added to an auction listing that she was forthcoming, finally admitting she'd been too embarrassed to tell him that she had been scammed and faced losing the house.

Viviana claimed she was a romantic, but she was also a grown woman who didn't need him lecturing her about the men she chose to become involved with; he'd hoped the imminent fear of finding herself homeless would finally allow her to think with her head and not her heart. A wry smile twisted his mouth when he recalled his mother claiming she was a romantic, hopelessly in love with her husband, and would stand by her wedding vows until death parted them. And it had.

Lee programmed the dishwasher and punched the start button. He then picked up his cell phone and tapped Angela's number. She answered after the third ring.

"Leland, come and get me!"

"What's wrong?" he asked, hearing panic in her voice.

"Please come."

His heart rate sped up. "Where are you?"

"I'm at Miss Joyce's."

"I'm on my way."

Lee hung up and dashed to the bedroom to retrieve his keys. He had never known Angela to be a drama queen, not even when she and Justin split up temporarily. She'd come to him and say, *"Justin and I are not speaking,"* and whenever they continued to share the lunch table she was the epitome of poise, not allowing anyone to suspect she and Justin were no longer a couple. But hearing her strident tone now had momentarily unnerved him. He wondered if something drastic had happened between her and her mother-in-law.

He wasn't overly fond of Joyce Mitchell and had never felt welcome in her home, but he respected her as

Justin's mother. Most times he'd suggested Justin and Angela come to The Falls House for their study sessions whenever it was Justin's turn to host the meetings. Miss Joyce, as people usually referred to her, used to glare at him and then turn her back without saying a word. It was apparent she sided with those in The Falls who believed he would end up like his father—a drug-addicted felon.

Lee tried not to overthink why Angela wanted him to come and get her as he managed to stay under the speed limit on his way to The Falls. Night had fallen over the landscape when he maneuvered up in front of the Mitchell house and spotted Angela waiting at the curb, clutching the handles of a Pullman. He got out of the jeep and came around to help her in at the same time the front door to the house opened and Joyce came down off the porch, gesturing wildly. He lifted the Pullman, storing it in the SUV's cargo area.

He closed the passenger-side door once Angela was belted in.

Angela's chest rose and fell heavily as she stared out the windshield. "You just got back and this is the second time I've burdened you with my problems. But I didn't know who else to call." She didn't have any close friends from high school, and had made it a practice not to discuss her personal business with coworkers.

Lee gave her a quick glance. "It's okay, Angie."

"Nothing is going to be okay until I finally move out and take control of my own life. When I told her that I was going to look for a house she went off on me, and I knew I couldn't spend another night under her roof without losing it completely. The woman knows exactly what buttons to push to make me lose it."

Decelerating, Lee rested his right hand on her denim-covered knee and gave it a gentle squeeze while steering with his left. "That's because she knows what to say to set you off."

Angela slowly shook her head. "She messes with me so much that I've learned to ignore her, especially when the kids are around, because I don't want them to see their mother go ballistic on their grandmother. She said something so twisted tonight that I knew I couldn't spend another minute there."

"Where do you want to go?"

She stared at Lee's distinctive profile. She had always thought him incredibly handsome, but his attractiveness didn't end there. He exuded a masculinity that was almost palpable. "I'd like to spend the night with you."

Lee's foot hit the brake, causing the vehicle to come to an abrupt stop. "No!"

Angela gave him an incredulous look. "Why not?"

"Because where I'm staying only has one bedroom."

"Do you have a sofa?"

"Yes."

"Then I'll sleep on your sofa. It'll be just for tonight." Angela wanted to tell Lee that she could check in to a hotel or motel, but she didn't want to be alone. Not tonight. And not when she needed to bare her soul about pretending to be strong when it was something she struggled with every day for the benefit of others *and* her children.

Lee exhaled an audible, ragged sigh. "Okay, Angela.

Just for tonight. If you need someplace to stay, then I'll call Vivi and have her put you up."

Angela clutched the hand on her knee. "I really appreciate it."

Lee pulled his hand away and activated the Bluetooth feature on the dash, connecting it to Viviana's number. "Hey, Vivi," he said when her greeting came on the speaker. "I have Angela with me and I'm asking if you can do her a favor."

"Of course. What does she need?"

"Can you prepare one of the bedroom suites for her? She'll be there tomorrow and she will let you know how long she's staying."

"That's not a problem. I'll put her in the suite across from mine. What about her twins?"

"They're away for the summer, so it'll just be her."

"No problem. Give her my number and have her call me before she comes over just in case I may have to step out."

"I will." He disconnected the call and met Angela's eyes. "You're all set."

Slumping against the leather seat, she nodded. "Thank you so much."

Chapter Four

Angela felt as if she could finally exhale after so many years of holding herself in check. Her appearance on the ramp had been touted as the next coming of supermodel Naomi Campbell, when in reality Angela had been just a frightened teenage girl who had to psych herself up before taking that first step onto the runway. And no one knew of her insecurities about her height and waif-thin body, which had become the brunt of jokes from her peers who called her Olive Oyl, the skinny cartoon character from *Popeye*. However, she had managed to hide her anxiety and lack of confidence whenever designers draped her frame with their latest creations and her stilettos hit the runway.

She willed her mind blank as Lee exited the interstate and turned onto a local tree-lined road. Seconds later he drove into the parking area of a three-story building, whose neon billboard identified it as an extended-stay residence. He pulled into a numbered space and shut off the engine.

"Don't move. I'll help you down after I get your bag."

Angela waited for him to get out and come around to assist her. He held the handles to the Pullman in one hand while his free arm went around her waist, lifting her effortlessly before setting her feet on the ground. She felt the calluses on the palm of his hand when he took hers in his and led her to the entrance of the hotel.

"I can remember when this building was a two-story motel." She couldn't tell Lee that it was the place where she had offered Justin her virginity. He had chosen it because it was located far enough away from Wickham Falls and off the road where they could hope for a modicum of secrecy. It was a day that had changed her life forever.

Lee smiled. "It's very different now."

"So I see," Angela said as she stepped into the updated lobby with several muted flat-screen televisions tuned to sports and all-news channels, contemporary tables, lamps and comfortable seating areas.

Lee nodded to the clerk at the front desk as they made their way to the elevators. "I'm on the third floor."

Walking into the elevator was like déjà vu for her, but instead of spending a few hours with her then boyfriend she would now spend the night with her best friend. Angela had lost count of the number of times she and Justin had broken up while in high school, but Lee had remained their constant. As their friend he didn't judge or interfere. She was aware he was dating a girl from his former school and she'd gotten to meet her for the first time at their senior prom. Cherise Williams was petite and shy, and claimed a flawless café au lait complexion. It was the first and last time Angela had seen Lee with another woman.

Lee swiped his keycard, opened the door and then stepped aside to let her enter, bowing slightly as if she were royalty. "*S'il vous plaît, entrez, madame.*"

Angela smiled. "*Merci.* You still speak French like a native. What other languages have you picked up during your travels?" She and Lee had shared French classes and she knew he had an uncanny gift for languages. By the time they graduated he was fluent in French and Spanish and had earned honors in both.

"Italian and Arabic."

Her eyebrows lifted. "Arabic?"

"Yep. I can speak, read and write it."

Angela wondered if he had utilized the language when deployed to the Middle East. "I'm really impressed."

She glanced around the open floor plan with a spacious living/dining area and galley kitchen. How different it was from the small room with a single bed, nightstand, chair, minuscule bathroom and closet where she and Justin had spent the afternoon making love. "Where are you going with my bag?" she asked Lee when he made his way down a narrow hallway.

"You can sleep in the bedroom tonight. I'll take the sofa. It converts into a queen-size bed," he said, smiling over his shoulder. "By the way, have you had supper?"

"Yes. I ate at a rest stop on the way back from Florida. But I could use a cup of coffee."

Lee stopped, but didn't turn around. "Same here."

"Do you mind if I make it?" she asked. She was tense and needed to do more than just stand around and watch Lee.

Lee glanced at her over his shoulder. "Of course not. The coffee maker is on the countertop and you'll find pods in the overhead cabinet to the left of the stove." He winked at her. "Now, do you remember how I like my coffee?"

She nodded. "A little milk and no sugar."

Lee smiled. "You do remember. You'll find a bottle of milk in the fridge."

Angela found the pods, dropped one into the well of the coffee maker and waited for it to brew as she examined the space that had become Lee's temporary home. She wondered why he had chosen to live in an extended-stay residence rather than the mansion where he had grown up. She was also aware, as with most in Wickham Falls, that Emory Remington had come back, but she didn't want to believe it was the reason why Lee had elected not to stay there. He'd never talked to her at length about his father, and she'd assumed he was either too embarrassed by or ashamed of the man.

"I love the smell of coffee any time of the day."

She turned to find that Lee had returned without making a sound—a feat she found remarkable for a man his size. There was no doubt it was a skill he'd developed as a member of Special Forces. At thirty he appeared in peak conditioning, which made him a magnificent masculine specimen. He'd brushed his hair and secured it in a man-bun.

"It's bacon for me." Breakfast was her favorite meal of the day.

Lee picked up her mug, handing it to her before grasping his. "Let's sit on the sofa where it's more comfortable."

He waited for Angela to sit before taking his seat beside her. Stretching out his legs, he crossed his feet at the ankles. "Tell me, why are you running away?"

Angela put the cup to her mouth and took a sip. "Is that what you think? That I'm running away?"

"Even if you move out and set up your own household, I doubt Miss Joyce is going to change. Which means it's up to you to change the narrative and your relationship with her."

Shifting slightly to face him, Angela met his eyes. "Why should I change, Lee? How many times do I have to ignore her accusations when she blames me for Justin losing his life?"

A frown creased his forehead. "That's crazy and you know it."

"Do I, Lee? Not when I have to hear it at least a couple of times a week. And if you do hear it enough you'll start to believe it."

Lee set his mug on the table, moved closer to Angela and rested his arm around her shoulders. "Joyce Mitchell is attempting to brainwash you to take the blame for something over which you or anyone had no control."

Angela laid her head on his shoulder. "She says I should've convinced Justin not to drop out of medical school and not to join the Marines."

"Didn't she know Justin never wanted to become a doctor? That it was her dream, not his."

"She would never admit that," Angela said in a quiet voice. "The first time I met Justin I overhead him tell Miss Joyce that he didn't want to be a doctor, but she was having none of what she'd call his crazy back talk."

Lee stared at a watercolor painting on the wall in

the dining area. "That's because she wants what she wants."

Angela sighed softly. "You're right about that."

Lee listened without saying a word as Angela related the conversation she'd had with her fiancé, who'd admitted he always wanted a career in the military; she told him once they were married he had her full support in whatever decision he made. When Justin had called and asked him to be his best man, Lee put in for leave and met the couple at the courthouse for the ceremony.

"Miss Joyce has always been intolerant and opinionated, which is why she's never had many friends," Lee said. "It's probably why her husband and son had become her whole world."

"And now that both are gone she's zeroed in on my children."

"What set her off this time?"

"I told her my parents were taking the kids to California and that when they return I plan to enroll Zoe and Malcolm in Miss Alma's Little Tots Childcare at the end of the summer." Angela paused, seemingly to compose herself. "That's when she said things to me I'd never repeat to anyone. I'm so done with her, Leland."

Lee knew Angela was upset whenever she didn't shorten his name. When he'd called and she said, *"Leland, come and get me!"* he'd known at once that she was in distress, although he never would've suspected she'd had a disagreement with her mother-in-law volatile enough to send her fleeing her home.

It was a long time ago that he, Justin and Angela had made a pact to remain friends for life, while he and Justin had pledged that they would always look out for Angela. It had been Justin that made him aware that many of the girls in their high school resented Angela because of her success as a teenage model. Her college professor parents only allowed her to take modeling assignments during summer and school holiday recess. Once she graduated, her career had skyrocketed and she'd earned the sobriquet of supermodel. Lee had come to recognize her vulnerability when she revealed to him that he and Justin were the only people she was able to trust to have her back.

It was at the reception following his wedding that Justin confided to Lee he wasn't returning to medical school, but had enlisted in the Corps and had two weeks before he was scheduled to report to Parris Island, South Carolina, for basic training. His mother had taken the news very hard and it was the reason she'd decided not to attend his wedding. Justin had thanked those who had come to help him celebrate one of the most important days in his life, unaware that two years later the same people would come together again, this time for his funeral.

"Enough talk about Miss Joyce," Lee said in a quiet voice. "I'm certain Viviana will let you live with her until you find a house."

Angela shifted again to face Lee. "What about you, Lee?"

He gave her an unwavering stare. "What about me?"

"When are you going to move into your home?"

She was asking a question to which he didn't have an answer. "I don't know."

"Is it because your father is back?"

Lee schooled his expression not to reveal his annoyance. First Viviana and now Angela wanted to talk about his relationship with his truant father. "I don't want to discuss him." His words were cold, harsh.

Angela recoiled as if struck across the face. "I didn't mean to pry."

Pressing a kiss to her forehead, Lee whispered, "Sorry for snapping at you, but if you don't mind I'd like to talk about anything other than our folks. Tell me about your new job."

Her expression brightened. "Last year I began working for Dr. Franklin as his receptionist. I was promoted to office manager after he took on a partner, Dr. Natalia Hawkins, who is amazing. She married Seth Collier last month."

"Vivi would mail me a batch of copies of *The Sentinel* to catch me up on the goings on in The Falls. When I read that Roger Jensen finally retired and the folks elected Seth as sheriff of Wickham Falls I felt they couldn't have picked a better lawman."

"Do you know what I'm noticing?" Angela asked.

"What's that?"

"That a lot of the guys that left to join the military have come back to stay. Sawyer Middleton now heads the technology department for the school district. He married one of their teachers. Then there's Aiden Gibson who also married a teacher. His girls now have a baby brother they spoil rotten. Of course you know about Seth." She paused. "Do you remember Mya Lawson?"

"Yes. Wasn't she voted the prettiest girl in her graduating class?"

Angela nodded. "I believe she was. She married Giles Wainwright, whose family owns and runs a major

New York real estate conglomerate. He was once a captain in the Corps."

Lee's curiosity was piqued at the mention of real estate. "Is he involved in real estate here in The Falls?"

"I'm not certain. But if you want I can introduce you to him. Mya brings her daughter into the clinic for checkups. Are you looking to buy property?"

"No. I'm looking to sell."

"Do you want me to contact her and tell him to call you?"

Lee smiled. "I'd appreciate it if you would."

He knew he had to get the ball rolling sooner than later about selling off some of the land to offset the cost of repairs and perhaps even renovations to the historic property. He wouldn't be able to ascertain the total cost until an engineer and architectural historian submitted their estimates. At this point he wasn't certain whether the house or the guesthouses were structurally sound.

"Are you going to sign up for the military challenge hosted by the American Legion and VFW during the Fourth of July three-day celebration?"

Lee angled his head. "Is that something new?"

"They'd planned it for last year, but the Chamber of Commerce had to cancel last year's festivities because there was so much rain that some of the valleys were flooded."

"Is it military against civilians?"

"No, no and no," she said, smiling. "That wouldn't be fair. It's only for present and former military."

There was nothing Lee liked better than a physical challenge. "It sounds like fun. Where do I sign up?"

"You can go to the Chamber office and add your

name to the list." Angela smothered a yawn with her hand. "Sorry about that."

Lee stood, extended his hand and pulled Angela to stand. "You should turn in. You've had a long day."

She managed a tired smile. "You won't get an argument out of me."

"There are towels and facecloths on a shelf under the vanity. Housekeeping changed the sheets this morning, so you have clean linen." Lee normally cleaned up after himself but requested housekeeping come three times a week to bring clean linen and towels and to dust and vacuum.

Going on tiptoe, Angela kissed his cheek. "Good night."

"Sleep tight," he teased.

Lee watched her walk, his gaze following the sway of her slender hips in the fitted jeans. Although she'd carried twins her body was fuller than it had been years ago. He had returned to his hometown to help his sister, unaware he would become involved in providing solace for his best friend's widow.

Lee had to remind himself that as much as he liked Angela and at one time had wanted more than friendship from her, he did not want to take advantage of her. She was waging an undeclared war with her mother-in-law and he had to be careful not to make a toxic situation worse. Joyce Mitchell wasn't above spreading vicious rumors that he was attempting to turn her daughter-in-law against her.

He waited for Angela to go into the bathroom and close the door before he retreated to the bedroom to get a change of clothes for the next day. He was an early riser and usually swam laps in the pool before starting his day.

Angela was still in the bathroom when he picked up the remote to the television and began channel surfing until he came to one recapping the day's sporting events. Lee lost track of time until he realized he'd reviewed the encore of the same game at least twice. He turned off the TV, removed the cushions from the sofa and pulled out the bed. He found an extra set of sheets, a lightweight blanket and pillows in the narrow utility closet, and made up the sofa bed.

He walked into the bathroom, encountering the lingering scent of Angela's bodywash. It had been a while since he had shared the same space with a woman, and that was something he sorely missed. Lee liked waking up to find a woman beside him or just lying in bed holding hands without either feeling the need to talk. He brushed his teeth and took a quick shower. Reaching for the robe on the back of the door, he slipped his arms into the sleeves. Lee normally slept nude, but he didn't want to shock Angela in case she walked in on him wearing only his birthday suit.

He extinguished all of the lights, leaving the one under the stove hood on, and then took off the robe and slipped into bed. The mattress on the sofa wasn't as thick as the one on his bed, but it was better than attempting to cram his six-three frame on a six-foot sofa. The only other alternative was sleeping on the floor.

Punching the pillow under his head, Lee managed to find a comfortable position as he closed his eyes. He thought about spending the day with his sister, and then Angela. Both had asked for his help. Viviana needed him to help her resurrect her business and Angela needed safe haven from her mother-in-law who hadn't gotten over grieving the loss of her only child. It was as if life had thrown Joyce Mitchell a curve not once but twice—she'd lost her husband as well as her son.

He did not want to think about Justin's mother or the man who'd scammed his sister. Instead, he wanted to focus on the promises he had made over the years: he had promised his mother that he would always look after his sister; promised Angela and Justin they would remain friends for life; and he'd promised Justin, as his best man, that he would be there and protect Angela if anything happened to him. Those were his last waking thoughts before he drifted off to sleep.

Angela woke and within seconds knew she wasn't in her own bed. Sitting up, she saw a monogrammed silver money-clip on the bedside table. Realization dawned as she recalled what had happened to send her running to Lee. Although she wasn't prone to bouts of melodrama, Angela felt as if she was a character in a daytime soap opera on television. It wasn't the first time she and Joyce had disagreed, but this time, she'd been particularly frustrated after the fatigue of driving nonstop for nearly twelve hours from Florida, cutting her vacation short by a week.

She'd just gotten used to getting up later than usual to while away hours in her parents' lanai or swim in their in-ground pool, while they assumed the responsibility of entertaining their grandchildren. However, her plan to do nothing more strenuous than breathe was interrupted when her mother had suggested taking Zoe and Malcolm to Los Angeles to visit their cousins. The die had been cast when Angela signed and notarized the necessary documents allowing her parents to travel with her children. Her father had suggested that she stay at the house for the duration of her vacation, but Angela had declined. She'd dropped her family off at the airport and continued northward to West Virginia.

The instant she walked through the door, she'd told Joyce she had come back early because her parents had taken the kids to California, and when they returned she was enrolling them in day care. What ensued was a litany of invectives that had rendered her temporarily mute. Turning on her heel, Angela had walked out and called Lee, knowing if she'd stayed it may have resulted in a physical confrontation. She had had enough of Joyce treating her as if she was some annoying insect or a thing no better than gum on the bottom of her shoes.

It was no longer about saving face in front of her children but maintaining a modicum of dignity and self-respect. Angela had been raised to respect her elders but it had become more and more difficult to do so living under the same roof with her mother-in-law. Viviana had agreed to let her stay at The Falls House and hopefully she wouldn't have to wear out her welcome before finding a house in town that would suit her needs and that of her children. And if she was able to secure a pre-approved mortgage then perhaps she would be able to close in time to enroll Malcolm and Zoe in day care.

Angela swung her legs over the side of the bed and as her feet touched the pale gray carpet she saw it. Walking to the door, she picked up the single sheet of paper. Lee had left her a note to say he had gone for a swim. Her stomach made a rumbling sound that reminded her that she hadn't eaten in sixteen hours. Lee had told her that she wasn't a guest and that meant she was free to raid his kitchen and prepare breakfast.

Lee felt invigorated from swimming laps in the Olympic-size indoor pool. He'd left a note for Angela in case she woke and found him gone. He swiped his keycard and opened the door to the tantalizing aroma of something sweet. He walked into the kitchen to find Angela barefoot in a black T-shirt over a pair of white leggings. She had covered her braided hair with a white bandanna. The scene of domesticity was like a punch in the gut. Now he knew what the men in the unit were talking about when they said they couldn't wait to get home to their wives.

Lee was one of a few who had remained single or didn't have a steady girlfriend. He'd found it difficult to form a lasting relationship with any woman because women always seemed to want to know about his childhood. They weren't content to accept that he had come from a broken home. He didn't want to explain that his father had deserted his family while his wife lay dying from an inoperable brain tumor. Talking about his past would dredge up memories he'd buried and didn't want to relive again.

"This is a scene I can really get used to. I wouldn't mind getting up every morning to a fabulous breakfast with homemade muffins."

Angela turned and smiled at him. "That's not happening, sport," she teased. "If you want what you call a fabulous breakfast every morning, then I'd expect an incredible supper every night. And please don't tell me you forgot how to cook because I remember you grilling the most delicious steaks I've ever eaten."

"Maybe that's something we can work on. Right now I need a shower and then I'll help you."

"I've got everything under control. All I have to do is cut up some fruit. Do you still like your eggs over easy?"

"Yes." It was apparent Angela hadn't forgotten a lot about his food preferences, while Lee hadn't been able to forget anything about her. And it had taken nearly a four-year absence for him to realize that every woman with whom he had become involved he had compared to Angela.

If he'd had to look up the word *friend* in the dictionary then Angela and Justin's names would be the definition. Both were loyal and uncompromising. It wasn't as if their relationship was without disagreements but it was never malicious. And from the moment Angela invited him to join her and Justin at their lunch table, a friendship had formed and cemented.

Lee stood under the spray of the showerhead, washing his hair as he reminisced about not maintaining close contact with Angela after he'd joined Special Forces. He wouldn't have been able to reveal where he was going or the mission to which his team had been assigned. He'd felt that he'd owed to his aunt and sister to let them know he was still alive. Becoming an elite soldier going out on covert missions made him aware of his mortality and there were instances when he second-guessed himself whether he wanted a wife and children to mourn his passing.

Viviana had asked him why he hadn't married and the answer was that the woman with whom he was in love was his best friend's widow.

He washed and rinsed his body, and wrapping a towel

around his waist, he went into the bedroom to dress. When he emerged Angela had set a bowl of sliced melon and strawberries on the table with a tray of blueberry muffins. She'd removed a platter of crisp bacon from the oven.

"I like a man who keeps a stocked fridge."

Lee walked over and kissed Angela's cheek. "That's because I like to cook."

She smiled at him. "That's where you differ from Justin. He couldn't boil an egg even if his life depended upon it. He claimed he didn't need to learn to cook when his mother was one of the best cooks and bakers in the county."

Lee knew Angela was right about Miss Joyce's baking prowess. Her cakes, pies and muffins had won a number of ribbons whenever there were baking competitions. He didn't tell Angela he didn't want to talk about Miss Joyce because he had offered her an alternative to living with her mother-in-law. She would move in with his sister, which would give her the space she needed to plan the future for her and her children.

He removed two mugs from the overhead cabinet. When he'd first checked into the suite he was pleasantly surprised to find place settings for four, small kitchen appliances, and cookware from muffin tins to baking sheets along with an assortment of sauces and frying pans.

Lee could easily become accustomed to sitting across from Angela and eating breakfast as if it was something they did every morning. They ate without talking while tunes from a station playing love ballads filled the suite. And each time he glanced up he saw Angela watching him. He wondered what was going on in her beautiful head.

"What are you thinking about?" he asked after a comfortable silence.

A mysterious smile parted Angela's lips. "How easy it is to get used to us having breakfast together."

His impassive expression concealed his innermost feelings. He was in love with Angela and he couldn't remember a time when he hadn't loved her. Even when he experienced guilt about coveting his best friend's girlfriend he had continued to love her from afar. Lee was able to distance himself emotionally once she became another man's wife, but seeing her again now that she was a widow, those feelings were back—this time stronger than ever.

"That can be arranged if you come over every once in a while."

Angela lowered her eyes. "Do I have to make a reservation?"

One of his eyebrows lifted slightly. "No. Why would you ask me that?"

"I don't want to intrude on you in case you have female company."

He leaned forward. "The only female company I anticipate having is you and Vivi." His answer seemed to satisfy Angela as she picked up her fork and pierced a piece of fruit. Her question about inviting a woman or women over made him wonder if she was perhaps jealous. He shook his head. That was only possible if her feelings for him went deeper than friendship, and he doubted whether she'd ever want more from him than companionship—something she could get from any man.

"As soon as you're finished I'll take you to get your car before you meet Vivi."

* * *

Angela felt as if she'd been doused with cold water. It appeared as if Lee wanted to get rid of her when she'd wanted to spend more time with him. There was something about his gentle manner that made her feel safe—safer than she ever had with Justin. Lee projected an inner strength that had allowed him to grow up to ignore the malicious gossip about his father. Not once had he broken—not even when the police accused him of burglary. Even after he was exonerated he refused to speak of the ordeal. He ranked in the top one percent of their graduating class and instead of going to college he'd joined the army.

Whenever he returned to The Falls, Angela found him changed. He'd become way more mature, confident and disciplined. The last time he came back it was for Justin's funeral, and he'd been an army ranger. And when he had to go through the most grueling test for the elite military forces, he'd succeeded where so many failed.

She met the large blue-gray eyes framed by thick black lashes, eyes that were so beautifully strange in a face that the sun had turned a rich mahogany. She examined the narrow bridge of his straight nose with slightly flaring nostrils and the firm lips that rarely parted in a smile. There were times when she wondered if he'd never learned to smile. And the few times she saw him smile she was transfixed because it seemed to light up his entire face.

Pushing back her chair, she stood, Lee rising with her. "As soon as I get my things I'll be ready to leave."

Chapter Five

Even before Viviana opened the massive oaken doors to allow her entrance Angela was aware of how much the Wolfe mansion had changed since her last visit, which now seemed eons ago. Even though the residence was no longer the Wolfe House but known as The Falls House after it was converted to a boardinghouse, Angela still thought of it by its former name.

The exteriors showed signs of obvious neglect, while the interiors reminded her of a woman who favored secondhand fashions from a bygone era. The rugs in the entryway were threadbare and the needlepoint cushions on the antique straight-back chairs bore signs of visible wear.

Viviana extended her arms and hugged Angela. "You're welcome to stay as long as you want."

Angela pressed her check to Viviana's. "Thank you, but you may come to regret saying that."

"I doubt it," Viviana said cheerfully. "Now that I've temporarily closed the boardinghouse, I could really use the company. My father left to go back to Philadelphia earlier this morning, which means there's just going to be the two of us for at least a couple of weeks. Come with me and I'll show you your bedroom." She glanced at Angela over her shoulder as they walked past the parlor into a great room and to the circular staircase leading to the second story. "Leave your bag here. I'll send it up in the dumbwaiter."

Angela followed Viviana up the staircase. Lee's sister had lost weight, as evidenced by the way her jeans were sagging around her slim hips. It was almost impossible to keep a secret in The Falls and people were taking bets as to when Viviana would marry her live-in boyfriend, because it had been a while since anyone had seen her with a steady man. However, the gossips were silenced when he abruptly moved out and subsequently Viviana announced she was closing the boardinghouse. Judging by her appearance it was evident the breakup hadn't been easy for her, and Angela wondered if the reason Lee had come back to Wickham Falls was to support her emotionally.

The runner on the second story landing had been removed and rolled up at the end of the hallway. It was the first time Angela had ventured upstairs in the house where she had come with Justin to study with Lee. They would gather either in what the Wolfes referred to as their drawing room or in the kitchen whenever Aunt Babs invited them to stay for supper. Its size never ceased to overwhelm her, and she'd always felt the appliances were better suited for a restaurant's commercial kitchen. Lee's aunt and uncle's decision to convert a wing of the house from a private residence to a boardinghouse was a no-brainer. The prior generation of Wolfes had closed their coal mines, which had not only diminished their wealth but also their standing as the most infamous family in Johnson County.

Viviana stopped and opened a partially closed door. "This is your bedroom, and I'm across the hall in case you need anything. I hope you like it."

Angela entered the room and held her breath. The elaborately carved antique mahogany king-size four-poster draped in sheer mosquito netting was the bedroom's focal point. She was drawn to the trio of floor-to-ceiling windows overlooking a veranda with views of verdant hills and mountains in the distance. The suite had everything she would want in a bedroom: en suite bath, a reading corner and a window seat with enough room to double as a daybed, and a round table with two pull-up chairs. She opened an armoire to find a flat-screen television.

Angela turned and smiled at Viviana. "I love it. Thank you so much."

Viviana returned her smile. "Don't thank me. Thank Lee. He's the one who suggested you stay here. I suppose it can't be easy living with Miss Joyce."

Angela went completely still, and wondered if Lee had told his sister about her dustup with her mother-in-law. "You know about us?"

"Girl, please," Viviana drawled. "Everyone knows she's a pain in the neck. I don't think she can get along with anyone more than five minutes, while you've been living with her for years. Anytime you need a break from her you're welcome to bring your adorable twins and hang out here. We still have a nursery with a connecting door from the master bedroom. It hasn't been used since I was a baby, so it's time for someone to occupy it."

Angela's eyelids fluttered as she attempted to hold back tears. Knowing she had someplace to go with her children if or when she found it impossible to continue to share the same roof with Joyce was something she couldn't have imagined before Lee returned to Wickham Falls. Her other alternative was accepting her parents' suggestion she live with them until she purchased a house in a nearby gated community.

She didn't want to leave The Falls, not only because Justin was buried in a section of the local cemetery set aside for veterans, but also because she wanted to raise her children in a small town. Even though her son and daughter would never get to know their father, Angela wanted them to hear from others that knew him that he was an honorable man.

Angela, like many others living in Wickham Falls, knew the town did have social problems, but fortunately not on the same scale as larger cities. The mayor, town council and the sheriff's department had developed an initiative to combat an increasing opioid epidemic sweeping the state.

"I'll give you a set of keys so you can come and go whenever you want. Do you have anything planned for today?" Viviana asked.

"I'm going to the bank to file for a pre-approved mortgage, and then head over to the real estate company to see what they have on their listings."

"What are you looking for?"

"A house that's turnkey and with at least four bedrooms. I want Malcolm and Zoe to have their own rooms and the extra bedroom can be for guests. Of course I want enough property for a backyard for the kids to play and if I want to eventually entertain."

Viviana pushed out her lips, seemingly deep in thought. "You should be able to find something on the other side of Pike Road."

Angela scrunched up her nose. Pike Road was across the tracks and many of the properties were run-down. "If I do find something there it will probably need a lot of work."

"The invitation still stands. You can always stay here until the work is completed."

She wanted to tell Viviana the last thing she wanted was to wear out her welcome. "I'll think about it," she said instead. "I'm going over to the bank to see the loan officer before it gets too crowded. When I come back we can go to Ruthie's for an early supper. My treat."

Viviana's golden brown eyes lit up like a child's on Christmas morning. "Better yet, let's go to the Wolf Den. Wednesday night is Ladies' Night and all drinks and appetizers are half price."

Angela nodded. "Count me in. I'll see you later." After she'd ended her career and married Justin, socializing had become a thing of the past. She no longer had contact with some of the women with whom she'd bonded when modeling. A few had gone on to become actresses, one or two married rock musicians, and the rest had settled down to become wives and mothers.

"Good luck."

Angela wanted to tell her the only luck she needed was finding a house in which to raise her children. She retraced her steps and walked out to get into her Honda Odyssey. It felt strange not to see the car seats in the second row. She'd given them to her parents to check at the airport for their flight to LA. Her brother's children had outgrown theirs and she wanted to spare her mother and father from having to purchase them while they were in California. Angela wasn't certain whether it was her imagination, but somehow the air smelled cleaner and the sun shone brighter as she headed in the direction of the business district.

Lee waited for the bank manager to bring him a bank check that would cover the delinquent property taxes. He'd done business with the same local bank for years. His military pay was direct-deposited into an account he had set up before leaving Wickham Falls.

The manager returned and handed him the check with an envelope. "Is there anything else I can do for you, Leland?"

He stared at the man he'd attended high school with. Gregg Jessup hadn't left The Falls to find work because his family owned several businesses, including the bank. "My certificate of deposit is maturing at the end of the month, and I've decided not to roll it over. I'll deposit the proceeds in my savings until I set up a business account."

Gregg smiled, exhibiting a mouth filled with large white teeth that had earned him the moniker of Toothy. "Are you planning to go into business for yourself?"

Lee knew he wouldn't be able to keep the plan to reorganize and reopen The Fall House as a B and B a secret for long, so he decided to tell Gregg the truth. After all, the man knew what he was worth down to the penny. The only exception was his retirement account he'd set up with a Fortune 500 investment company.

He'd recommended operating a bed-and-breakfast because it was more cost-effective They would offer one meal instead of two, and revenue derived from charging for a daily room rate was higher than weekly or even monthly rates. And the overall expenses for B and B lodgers would be lower from those permanently living in the house: food, utilities, and laundry, and housekeeping duties.

Gregg sobered. "I'm glad you're helping out your sister," he said under his breath as if they were coconspirators. "As quiet as it's kept, only I know about her stolen identity. And I do feel somewhat responsible because I should've flagged certain transactions that looked rather suspicious. However, it was when she overdrew her line of credit that the warning bells went off. And when she came in and I showed her that her boyfriend had attempted to purchase a late-model, top-of-the-line BMW, she started talking about finding him and blowing him away, and I literally had to talk her off the roof. It was a side of Viviana I've never seen before and don't want to see again."

A wry smile twisted Lee's mouth. "She does have a quick temper." He extended a hand. "Thanks, Gregg."

Gregg took the proffered hand. "No problem, Leland. Let me know if you need anything else."

Lee stood up. "I will." As he turned to walk out of the bank he nearly collided with Angela. His hands went out to steady her. "Sorry about that."

Her head came up. "I should be the one apologizing. I wasn't looking where I was going."

His eyes lingered on her face. "Did you settle in okay?"

Her eyes lowered demurely. "Yes. The suite is perfect."

Lee dropped his hands. "Good. I guess I'll see you around."

She smiled. "I'm certain you will."

I know I will, Lee thought as he walked out into the bright summer sun. He had thought his feelings for Angela would have diminished over the years, but to his surprise they were back—stronger than before. What he had to figure out was what he was going to do about it.

Lee wanted to make one more stop before driving to the county seat to pay the back taxes. He walked two blocks to the building housing the Chamber of Commerce. An elderly woman with blue hair peered at him over her half-glasses.

"May I help you, sonny?"

Lee bit back a smile. He hadn't been called sonny in a very long time. "Yes. I'm here to sign up for the Legion and VFW military challenge."

Her eyes narrowed. "Did anyone tell you that there's a fee of one hundred dollars? The money goes to a fund for retired veterans who need assistance with living expenses or medical equipment. You can donate more if you wish, and we do accept credit cards."

Reaching into the pocket of his jeans, Lee took out a card and slid it across the counter. "Double it, and where do I sign?" He didn't mind being generous for a good cause. She handed him a clipboard where twenty-four others had signed up. He jotted down his name, branch of service, active or inactive, rank and email.

She processed his card and returned it to him. "Thank you." Her eyes narrowed. "I thought I recognized you, but I didn't want to call you out of your name. Don't you remember me?"

Lee shook his head. "No, ma'am."

"I used to work in the middle school cafeteria."

"I didn't attend The Falls Middle School. I transferred over my first year in high school."

"I want to thank you for your service and generous donation." She glanced at the clipboard again. "You did real well, Sergeant Remington. You're the first army ranger to sign up."

He smiled. "Thank you."

"I want you on my team for the tug-of-war," drawled a voice Lee hadn't heard in years.

He shifted to find Aiden Gibson standing behind him. Aiden was a few years older than Lee and was one of the few local boys who'd joined the navy. Most went into the army or the Marines. Vivi had told him that at last year's Memorial Day celebration Aiden had proudly worn his trident pin for the first time.

Lee offered the former SEAL his hand, but Aiden ignored it and pounded Lee's back. "If we're on the same team, then folks are going to accuse us of taking advantage of our brothers in arms because we were Special Forces."

Aiden laughed. "They can think whatever the hell they want. This is a challenge and I don't like losing." Even though his mouth was smiling, his blue-green eyes were serious. Although he'd left the navy years ago he'd continue to wear his blond hair in a military style.

"I hear that you're now a new poppa."

Aiden pressed large hands to his chest. "I got my boy. My girls carry him around as if he were a doll."

"What about his mama?"

A flush suffused the face of the Wolf Den's pit master. "She's incredible. I never thought I'd get married again, but Taryn's my queen. Why don't you come by the Den tonight? I'm certain some of the guys will be glad to see you, because there was talk that you were coming back last year."

"I'd planned to but something came up."

"Something like a mission?"

Lee nodded. "Yep."

"You got a special girl?"

Unconsciously Lee's brow furrowed. "No. Why?"

"Because tonight is Ladies' Night at the Den and maybe you'll meet someone. The women come from Mineral Springs and a few other towns all over the county."

He wanted to tell Aiden he wasn't looking to meet someone when the person he was interested in was currently staying with his sister. "I'll definitely stop by."

Aiden pounded Lee's shoulder again as he resisted the urge to wince. It was apparent the man didn't know his own strength. Aiden didn't like losing and neither did Lee. If they were given the option of choosing teams, then he would pick the former SEAL's.

He left the Chamber and walked to the parking lot behind a row of buildings to retrieve his vehicle. As soon as he paid the back taxes Viviana could exhale knowing she wouldn't have to lose her ancestral home.

Angela checked her reflection in the mirror and smiled. She couldn't believe she was going out at night—even if it was to a local sports bar and barbecue joint. She and Viviana had agreed they weren't going to the Wolf Den to hook up with anyone, but they just wanted to have fun.

Once she had returned from the real estate office, she'd spent the better part of an hour undoing her braided hair before washing the chemically straightened strands, blowing it and securing it in a ponytail. She had opted for the braided hairstyle to save time. Now that she was working she had little time to devote to herself. Most of her time away from work went into taking care of her children. Although Joyce watched Malcolm and Zoe when she was at work, Angela insisted on getting the twins up, bathing and getting them dressed before breakfast. And weekends were devoted to spending as much time with them as possible. She managed to get a hair appointment, manicure and pedicure whenever she could—which wasn't too often. A few times she'd paid her stylist to come to her home to do her hair.

Viviana had been forthcoming about her breakup with her last boyfriend. Not only had he taken out credit cards in her name but he had also had someone duplicate her social security card and birth certificate, while he'd become adept at forging her signature. And he must have had a female accomplice who looked a lot like her so he could use a photo ID in Viviana's name. Angela laughed when Viviana told her she'd posted his photo on as many social media sites as she could, in order to warn women to be wary of him because he trawled dating sites for unsuspecting marks.

Viviana's mood had changed, becoming somber, when she admitted having to file for bankruptcy and alert credit monitoring companies that she had become a victim of identity theft. Angela had tried to reassure her that he would eventually get caught and sent to prison.

Angela looked at herself in the mirror again. She had decided to wear a pair of black stretchy pants with cuffs that showed her ankles. She had changed her blouse twice, finally deciding on a long-sleeved black boat-neck top in the same fabric as her slacks.

She did not have much of a choice when it came to footwear. She'd left Joyce's house wearing the running shoes she'd worn on her trip back from Florida. In her Pullman, she'd packed several pairs of sandals for her vacation and one pair of dress shoes in case she was going to an upscale restaurant with her parents. Bending over, she now slipped her bare feet into a pair of black slingback stilettos.

A light knock on the bedroom door garnered her attention. "Come in."

Viviana walked in and stopped short. "Well, look at you, Miss Supermodel Extraordinaire. Now I see why you were paid the big bucks for working the runway. Girl, you've still got it."

"Wearing spandex is a far cry from haute couture."

"Spandex or raw silk, you're the perfect human on which to hang clothes," Viviana said, grinning. She pointed to Angela's left hand. "Are you going to take those off?"

She looked down at her fingers. "No."

Viviana ran her hand over her hair. "You can tell me it's none of my business, but are you trying to keep men at a distance by making them believe you're married?"

Angela stared at Lee's sister. To say she was beautiful was an understatement. Whether she wore her hair in a mass of black curls, straight, or in waves as she did now, she was definitely someone men could not ignore. She was average height for a woman, and before her recent weight loss, her body would have been described as lush with curves in all of the right places. Her large golden brown eyes looked as if she was perpetually smiling. Tonight she wore a pair of stretch jeans, a white silk man-tailored shirt and three-inch navy leather pumps. She'd rolled back the cuffs of the shirt to reveal a number of colorful African and Native-American-inspired beaded bracelets on both wrists.

"I wear my rings because in my heart I'm married to Justin."

"Does that mean you'll never marry again?"

"That's not what I'm saying. If I meet someone and fall in love with him I'll definitely be open to marrying again, but only if he's willing to accept me *and* my children. We come as a package deal."

Viviana smiled. "Good for you. I didn't know Justin that well, but I'm willing to bet he didn't want you to spend the rest of your life in mourning if anything happened to him."

Angela didn't know if Viviana was clairvoyant, because those were the exact words he'd said to her when he received his orders that he was to be deployed.

She nodded. "You're right. But tonight we're not going to pick up men but have some fun."

Viviana launched into a raucous rendition of Cyndi Lauper's "Girls Just Want to Have Fun," and Angela joined her as she picked up her cross-body purse.

Lee walked into the Wolf Den and couldn't help smiling when he saw a banner stretched over the bar: *WELCOME HOME US ARMY RANGER SERGEANT*

LELAND WOLFE REMINGTON. He endured slaps on his back and handshakes until a piercing whistle rent the air.

Aiden, wearing a chef's blouse over a pair of black-and-white checkered pants, waved his hands above his bandanna-covered head for silence. "When I ran into Sergeant Remington earlier this morning and invited him here I thought he wouldn't show up. Now that he's here, you dudes have to show him some love."

Lee glanced at the men and women standing two- to three-deep at the bar, finding it odd that he had to wait until he was thirty to be accepted by those in his hometown. "Petty Officer Gibson should know army rangers never cut and run."

Those who'd served in the army cheered loudly as some sang the marching cadence, "Here We Go Again." Feeling buoyed, Lee launched into "Fired Up," the workout to the running pace of the US Army Rangers, with everyone echoing the chants.

Someone handed him a mug of ice-cold beer and he took a deep swallow. This was what he loved and missed about the military: the camaraderie that made men and women who served a special breed. It wasn't until he turned and placed the empty mug on the tray of a passing waitress that he noticed Angela and his sister standing in the doorway. He didn't know how long they'd been there watching the antics, but he was glad to see them.

He pushed his way through the crowd and found himself unable to pull his gaze away from Angela's face. Smoky shadow on her lids and a raspberry color on her lush mouth accentuated her best features. Leaning closer, he brushed a kiss over her cheek. The out-

line of her body in the black garments and the subtle
scent of her perfume snared him with a spell of longing he had not thought possible. He repeated the gesture with Viviana.

"I never expected to see the two of you tonight."
He had to raise his voice to be heard over the sounds
of escalating revelry.

Angela pressed her mouth to his ear. "Viviana said
it's Ladies' Night, so I decided to come with her and
check it out."

Lee smiled at her. "I'm glad you did. Let me see if
I can get you a table or a booth." It wasn't quite seven
and the Wolf Den was filled to near capacity. He motioned to get Aiden's attention.

"What's up?" Aiden asked.

"I need a table for my sister and Angela."

Aiden craned his neck. "I'll get someone to shift a
couple of tables to make room for them. Meanwhile
have Sharleen take their orders."

For Lee it appeared as if nothing had changed in
his absence. Sharleen Weaver still waited tables in the
family-owned-and-operated eating establishment. He
knew kids who couldn't wait to turn twenty-one to
drink, because the Wolf Den was the only place in The
Falls licensed to serve alcohol.

Another shout went up and Lee recognized Sawyer
Middleton, who'd also joined the army. "Where's my
fellow army buddy?" Sawyer shouted.

Lee excused himself and went to greet Sawyer and
gave him a rough hug. Sawyer was several years ahead
of him in high school, and the Middletons, like the
Wolfes, claimed roots that were recorded before West
Virginia achieved statehood.

"How did you know to show up here?" Lee asked Sawyer. He was as surprised as many residents had been when the software engineer returned after a stint in the military and subsequently established a successful company in New York before deciding to come back and settle down in The Falls.

"Aiden sent out an email to everyone military, whether active or inactive."

Lee wondered how Aiden was able to pull the gathering together so quickly, including printing the colorful banner. "How long did it take you to adjust to life as a civilian?"

Sawyer signaled to one of the bartenders for a beer. "It was easy because I hadn't planned to be a lifer. What about yourself?"

Before Lee could answer, a deep voice shouted, "Hoorah!"

"Damn," Sawyer swore under his breath. "Some jarhead just walked in."

Throwing back his head, Lee laughed loudly. It was apparent Sawyer wasn't too fond of marines. "There's a lot of them in the house tonight."

Lee's smile was still in place when he came face-to-face with Sheriff Seth Collier. The former military police master sergeant had joined the Corps within weeks of graduating high school much to the disappointment of his father, who'd expected him to join the family's general contracting company. Seth had campaigned for sheriff of Wickham Falls, won in a landslide, and he had also made history as the first African American to hold the office.

Seth rested his hands on Lee's shoulders. "Nice," he drawled. "You've done The Falls proud, Leland. Let me know if you want to go into law enforcement. I can put in a good word for you with the sheriff over in Mineral Springs who is looking for someone with your skills."

Lee's smile slowly slipped away. "I'll keep that in mind." He didn't tell Seth that he planned to reenlist and that his stay in Wickham Falls had an expiration date. "By the way, congratulations on your recent marriage."

Seth flashed a sheepish grin. "Thanks, man."

"Attention!"

Lee and the others in the sports bar snapped to attention and affected a snappy salute when a tall man with raven-black hair and electric blue eyes walked in. "At ease," he ordered, grinning from ear to ear as a number of rolled up paper napkins were thrown at him.

"Aren't you overdoing it, Captain Wainwright?" Seth shouted.

Lee remembered Angela telling him that a Wainwright was involved in real estate and he'd married local girl Mya Lawson, and he wondered if he was the same man. Folding his arms over his chest, he angled his head and watched as the captain shook hands and patted backs like a candidate campaigning for office until he stood in front of Lee. He offered him his hand.

"I'm honored to meet you, son."

Lee shook his hand. "Thank you, Captain."

"It's Giles. I was Captain Wainwright in a former life."

"Were you in the Corps?"

Giles affected a smug grin. "What else is there?"

Lee rolled his eyes upward. "What's up with you marines? You act as if you guys are the only branch in the service."

Giles leaned in close. "I have to perpetuate the hype.

Though I never would've been able to survive the rigorous training to become a ranger, Delta Force or a SEAL, which means I give you dudes props for becoming elite soldiers."

"I know this is not the time to discuss business, but I was told you're into real estate and I have some land I'd like to sell off."

"I handle international properties for the company, but I can contact my cousin Noah Wainwright, who's involved in the domestic sales. Currently he's involved in a development project in DC that may tie him up for the next month. I'll let you know when he's available to come down and meet with you."

Lee smiled again. "I'd appreciate that."

"What can I get you, Captain Wainwright?" one of the bartenders called out.

"Whatever you have on tap," Giles said.

"What about you, Leland? Do you want another brew?"

"Nah, Fletcher. I'm good." He excused himself and went to see if his sister and Angela were seated, and had placed their orders.

Chapter Six

Angela forced a smile she did not quite feel as Lee approached her table. She thought about how much Justin would've enjoyed being there to help the others celebrate Lee's homecoming. Guilt assailed her when the thought popped into her head what if the circumstances were reversed and it was Justin they were welcoming home instead of Lee. What if her husband's best friend had had a military funeral and Justin had been his pallbearer instead of the other way around?

The brittle smile faded, replaced by one filled with inviting warmth as she stared at the man who, along with many of the men and women in the restaurant, had risked his life to protect their country. Lee did appear tall, dark and dangerous dressed all in black: a long-sleeve mock V-neck cotton tee, slacks and boots. There wasn't an inch of excess fat on his tall, lean body. She found herself transfixed watching him smile whenever someone greeted him. He'd smiled more in the span of twenty minutes than she'd ever seen him. It was apparent he loved all things military and that interacting with those who'd served had given him what he was unable to find in Wickham Falls: acceptance.

Lee sat next Angela. "Did you order?"

Viviana nodded. "Sharleen took our order."

"What are you drinking?" he asked.

"I ordered a green apple martini," Angela said, "and Viviana a Long Island Ice Tea."

Lee whistled softly. "A Long Island Ice Tea can be lethal. I hope you're not the designated driver, Vivi."

Viviana scrunched up her nose. "Angela's driving tonight." She pushed back her chair. "Excuse me, but I'm going to get our drinks."

Lee rose to stand. "I'll help you."

"Stay," Viviana urged. "I've got this."

Draping an arm over the back of Angela's chair, Lee leaned close. "I forgot to tell you that you look amazing."

Angela lowered her eyes. There was something in Lee's voice that sent a shiver of awareness racing through her body like a lit fuse. "Thank you."

His mouth touched her ear. "No need to thank me for stating the truth."

She closed her eyes. His warm breath, the hypnotic scent of his aftershave and his low, sensual voice made her aware that it had been much too long since she'd been reminded she was a woman—a very passionate woman with physical needs that needed to be assuaged.

She slowly turned her head until their noses were inches apart. Staring into the blue-gray eyes made her feel as if she was looking into the sky with angry storm clouds in the distance.

Angela was certain Lee could hear her heart pounding in her chest. When she and Justin occasionally broke up and she would continue to interact with Lee, she'd asked herself if she had chosen to date the wrong boy. Lee was steadfast in his friendship, while Justin often proved to be unpredictable. And she blamed that on his mother. He'd denied himself to please his mother and that made their relationship erratic and unstable. Even Justin's decision to drop out of medical school to join the military had caused a rift in their relationship when Angela told him he'd wasted time and money pursuing something he didn't want. But in the end she had supported him because she loved him.

"Whenever I broke up with Justin I tried imagining what it would be like to date you."

Easing back, Lee gave her a long, penetrating stare. "If we had dated I know I would've asked you to marry me."

Angela glanced away. The intensity in Lee's eyes frightened her. "And our lives would've been very different."

"No doubt. I'm not certain whether we would've had twins, and you definitely wouldn't have had Miss Joyce as a monster-in-law."

Angela laughed in spite of the seriousness of their conversation. She had been widowed for four years, and giving birth months after burying her husband had been the most vulnerable time in her life. If Lee had proposed marriage, she probably would have accepted it, as a recent widow and new mother.

It wasn't easy living with Joyce, but Angela had no

intention of using Lee as an excuse to escape her calculating, domineering mother-in-law. "What is it exactly that you want from me?"

"I want you to allow me to fulfill the promise I made to Justin before we graduated. That I would take care of you if anything ever happened to him."

"So, this is all about you keeping a promise to a dead man?"

"That's not the only reason."

"What's the other, Lee?"

"It's how I feel about you."

"And what's that?"

A muscle twitched in Lee's jaw. "We're friends but I want more from you than friendship."

She stared at him. "What I don't understand is you sending me double messages."

"We're not who we were high school, Angela. I'm talking about us dating."

"I…" Her words trailed with Viviana's approach. "We'll talk about this later."

Lee lowered his arm and sat straight. "Come over for breakfast tomorrow morning."

"I can't. I have an appointment with Mrs. Riley at the realty company to see a few houses."

Angela sandwiched her hands between her knees to conceal their shaking. She wanted to believe Lee was teasing her, that he'd changed so much that she no longer knew the real Leland Remington. And that he'd become a master at concealing his emotions. The strained mood was shattered when she saw Viviana balancing two glasses with their cocktails.

Viviana set the drinks on the table, which had place settings for four. "Fletcher said he was going to have someone bring the drinks to the table but I told him we didn't want to wait." She stared at Angela, and then Lee. "What did I miss?"

"Nothing," Angela and Lee said in unison.

"If you say so," Viviana drawled. "Aren't you drinking anything?" she asked her brother.

"I had a beer. Right now I need to eat."

As if on cue, Sharleen appeared balancing a tray on her shoulder. She set out serving dishes with pulled pork, barbecue spare ribs, brisket, coleslaw, potato salad, baked beans and cornbread. "Enjoy!"

Angela stared at the food. "I think we ordered too much."

A shadow fell over the table. "Do you guys mind if I join you?"

"Please do, Sawyer," Angela urged. "How's Jessica and the baby?"

Sawyer set his plate on the table and sat next to Viviana. "They're both good now that James is sleeping throughout the night."

"The Falls is currently experiencing a population explosion," Angela said to Lee, as she filled her plate with pulled pork, baked beans and coleslaw.

He smiled. "Maybe one of these days our census will make it past five thousand."

"That's really a stretch unless women start having multiple births."

"Don't look at me," Angela said in protest when three pairs of eyes were directed at her. "I nearly fainted when Dr. Franklin told me I was carrying twins."

"Maybe if you get pregnant again you'll have triplets," Viviana teased.

Angela took a sip of her drink rather than reply to

Lee's sister's taunt. Fortunately a roar went up from the assembly whenever another veteran arrived at the homecoming celebration, redirecting the attention from her to Lee. She had noticed a number of women staring at Lee as they passed their table. Some she recognized from high school. They were the girls who'd been warned by parents to stay away from him. Oh, she mused, how times had changed. Not only hadn't Lee followed in his father's footsteps to serve time in prison, but had served his country as an elite soldier.

Sawyer pushed back his chair. "I'm going to get another beer. Do you want one, Lee?"

Lee stood up. "I'll join you." He nodded to Angela, and then Viviana. "Excuse us, ladies."

Viviana shook her head. "I think they've had enough of the so-called ladies' section and would rather bond with the dudes at the bar."

Angela smiled. "I agree."

She didn't know if it was a tradition on Ladies' Night, but the women tended to congregate in the rear of the restaurant rather than at the bar. However, observing the camaraderie between the men who'd shared a bond because they'd served their country, she recalled the times when Justin returned home on leave more animated than she'd ever seen him in his life. All he talked about was the Corps and the men and women whom he considered his military family. Then his mood would change whenever he expressed regret in taking so long to discover he'd always wanted a military career—a career that had eventually cost him his life.

Angela took a sip of her martini, enjoying the slightly sour apple flavor on her palate before it slid down her throat and warmed her chest. She was glad Viviana had suggested they go out because it offered her a glimpse of what she'd been missing since becoming a wife and mother. When she'd shared a flat with other models in Paris and Milan they rarely went out socially, and definitely not to eat. Most of the girls acted as if it was a mortal sin if they ate a full meal, while Angela discovered she could eat whatever she wanted and not gain weight, which she attributed to a high metabolism. Breakfast for other women was plain yogurt with a sprinkling of granola and berries. They drank gallons of water because coffee or tea tended to stain their teeth. It was salad for lunch and protein and steamed vegetables for dinner. Cake, bread and pasta were no-nos.

When she made the decision to leave modeling it was not with regret. She'd returned home to Wickham Falls and reconnected with Justin. They picked up with each other as if time and distance had not been a factor, and when he proposed marriage she accepted. She knew her parents wanted her to have a wedding with a gown, flowers and bridesmaids, but Angela had had enough of public displays of pomp and pageantry when walking the runway, and had opted for a simple ceremony at the local courthouse.

"Are you okay?"

Angela blinked as if coming out of a trance when she heard Viviana. "Yes. Why?"

"You looked as if you'd zoned out for a minute."

She decided to be truthful when she said, "I was just thinking about when I was a model."

Viviana rested her elbow on the table and cupped her chin on the heel of her hand. "Do you miss it?"

"No."

"Is it as glamorous as it appears?"

Angela shook her head. "No," she repeated. "Not when I had to put up with egotistical, neurotic designers who'd abuse their workers if a garment didn't fall at the exact angle on a model. Once I knew I was getting out of the business I gave one a piece of my mind and he was so shocked that anyone would speak to him in that manner that he was mute for a full minute. Then I gathered my things and walked out as his workers blew me kisses and a few had silently applauded. If I hadn't feared getting arrested in a foreign country for assault, I definitely would've slapped his arrogant face."

Viviana laughed. "It's good you didn't."

"I came along at the right time and booked a lot of go-sees because black models were suddenly in demand and I was able to make a lot of money, most of which I've saved." Angela stared at Lee as he shared a laugh with someone. "I've never seen Lee smile this much."

Viviana shifted her chair until she faced the bar. "That's because he's with his band of brothers. My brother eats and sleeps anything connected to the military."

A slight frown appeared between Angela's eyes. "What's the attraction? Is it the uniform or the weapons?"

"Don't start me lying, Angela, because I couldn't begin to explain it."

"Other than health care and college tuition it must hold some other appeal or many boys who leave The Falls wouldn't join the military."

Viviana met Angela's eyes. "Remember recruiters from all the branches come here during the high school's career week with offers that make it hard for the boys and some girls to refuse. Hypothetically, if there's a graduating class of ninety, then at least one-third of them sign up to serve. There were always jobs for boys who wanted to become coal miners like their fathers and great-grandfathers before the Wolfes decided to close the mines rather than install the government-mandated safety measures."

Angela stared at the food on her plate. Viviana and Lee were descendants of the family who preferred profits over safety for their employees, and those with long memories were quick not to let them forget it. The Wolfe children did not attend the public schools but were enrolled in military, parochial or prep schools before going onto and graduating from elite colleges. The tradition had ended when Lee transferred to the local high school, while Viviana graduated her private school and then enrolled in the University of Virginia.

"Does it bother you that folks still think of you and Lee as Wolfes?"

Angela had asked the question and wondered if some of the townsfolk would paint her with the same broad brush if she married Lee. "It doesn't bother me, but I don't know about my brother. Lee's not one to open up about his feelings."

She wanted to tell Viviana she was wrong. It had taken more than a decade, and she was still attempting to recover from Lee's revelation he sought more from her than friendship when he'd mentioned dating. What Angela did not want to do was use him to escape her current situation. Yes, she was living in his home and hoped it would only be temporary. Milly Riley had made arrangements to show her several properties within her price range.

Angela wanted to purchase property before her children returned to Wickham Falls, which meant she had five weeks in which to find a house. "Lee has always been the strong, silent type," she quipped.

"Stubborn is more like it," Viviana countered. "Once he decides not to talk about something you can consider it moot." She closed her eyes. "I think this Long Island Ice Tea is getting the best of me."

"I'm ready to leave whenever you are." They'd spent more than an hour at the restaurant. Angela signaled for one of the waitresses to bring the check.

The young woman who was related to the owners and barely looked old enough to drink shook her head. "Sharleen told me Sergeant Remington will cover your check."

Angela was slightly taken aback with the news. "If that's the case, then I'll leave the tip."

"I can't accept it. Sergeant Remington is the guest of honor and my uncle would disown me if I took money from his wife."

Wife! Angela stared with wide, unblinking eyes. Where did the waitress come up with the notion that she was married to Lee? "Sergeant Remington and I aren't married."

A noticeable flush suffused the woman's cheeks. "Please forgive me. Because you were sitting together and you're wearing wedding rings I'd assumed you were married."

"There's nothing to forgive. Good night, and let Aiden know everything was delicious."

"I heard what she said about you and Lee," Viviana said quietly as they wended their way through the crowd to the door. "Too bad it isn't real."

"Don't even go there, Viviana. It's not going to happen." Viviana gave her a look that Angela interpreted as meaning she didn't believe her. There was no way she was going to marry Lee without first dating him. She liked him—a lot, and wanted them to spend more time together before marriage even became an issue.

They were only feet from the door when Lee appeared. "Where are you going?"

Viviana rested a head against her chest. "I'm feeling a little woozy."

He shook his head. "I told you that drink would have you on your bottom." He ruffled her hair. "Come on, I'll walk you to your car."

"Hey, Dark Knight," someone shouted. "Where are you going?"

Lee glanced over his shoulder. "I'm going to walk my girls to their car to make certain some of you cretins don't accost them."

"Hurry back, Batman. We still have to choose up teams for the challenge."

Angela chuckled under her breath as she walked to where she'd parked her Honda. There wasn't an empty space in the lot, leaving drivers to park in a grassy area under a copse of trees. "I didn't know you were an action hero," she said to Lee as he opened the passenger-side door for Viviana and helped her up.

Lee leaned inside the minivan and snapped his sister's seat belt. "I also have special powers no one knows about."

Viviana waved Lee away. "Please stop talking so Angela can get me home before I'm sick."

"Close the door, Lee," Angela ordered at the same time she started the engine and quickly maneuvered out of the space. She stole a glance at Viviana, who'd reclined the seat and closed her eyes. The Long Island Iced Tea was made with at least five liquors that Viviana had drunk much too quickly, while as the designated driver Angela had only taken a couple of sips of her martini. She managed to drive back to The Falls House in record time and when she unlocked the door to the historic residence Viviana bolted inside and up the staircase.

Angela wanted to tell her host that she should follow Lee's lead and drink beer or wine, and not an alcoholic concoction with at least five different spirits that didn't remotely resemble tea. She decided to give Viviana the privacy she needed to cope with her discomfort before checking on her.

Angela groaned inwardly as she walked in and out of rooms that appeared to be no larger than the closets in the house where she'd grown up. And she wouldn't be able to fit more than a queen-size bed and bedside table in the so-called master.

"This house is smaller than the last one," she said to the Realtor who'd been carefully monitoring her response to the properties she'd elected to show her.

Milly Riley adjusted her horned-rimmed glasses and affected a professional smile. "It's small but move-in ready."

Angela stared at the middle-aged woman with shimmering silver hair who'd obviously been nipped and tucked and had nearly three decades of real estate experience. She was neatly dressed and had paired a navy blue silk blouse with a lemon yellow linen pantsuit. "It's still too small for me and my children. I want a house where I don't have to look for another place once they become teenagers and perhaps have sleepovers."

"I have a few more listings, but they may exceed your budget."

"I'm willing to spend a little more to get what I want." Angela had given the Realtor a figure, but it wasn't written in stone.

Milly nodded. "I have a client who's planning to relocate to Texas in October and their house would probably be perfect for you and your children. The property's address is Wickham Falls but its location puts it within the Mineral Springs school district."

Angela shook her head. "I'm not going to pay Wickham Falls' school tax and then send my kids to another school district."

"I understand your reluctance, Mrs. Mitchell. But before you write it off I'd like you to see the property for yourself. You just may change your mind. The owners are away and won't be back until the second week in July. Meanwhile, I'll line up some other properties for you to see after the Fourth of July fair."

"Okay." Not only did Angela have a problem sending her son and daughter to another school district but she also didn't want to wait until October to move in. "I'll wait for your call after the holiday."

Ten minutes later Angela pulled into the driveway to the house where she'd spent more than three years in a power struggle with her mother-in-law. She hadn't talked to Joyce since the evening she walked out and spent the night with Lee.

Joyce stood up as she walked into the living room.

"I suppose you're back now that you've finished tramping with that Wolfe boy."

Angela had promised herself nothing Joyce could say would get a rise out of her. "I've come back to get the clothes I need for work," she said with a smile.

Joyce's jaw dropped. "You're not staying?"

"No."

"What have I done to deserve this ungratefulness?"

Opening her handbag, Angela took out her checkbook, wrote a check payable to Joyce Mitchell and scrawled her name on the signature line. She placed the check on a side table. "That should be more than enough to take care of the house's expenses for a while."

Walking into her bedroom, Angela removed garments from the closet and dresser drawers and piled them on the bed. She filled three large weekenders with clothes that would last throughout the summer and fall. Looping the handles of two of them over her shoulders, she managed to carry the other one without too much difficulty.

"You must really hate me to treat me like this," Joyce said tearfully when she entered the living room.

Angela stopped and gave her children's grandmother a long, penetrating stare. "I don't hate you, Miss Joyce. In fact I love you as much as I love your son and his children. And because I want to continue to love you I realize we can't live together. You fail to understand that I'm an adult and I don't want my kids to grow up seeing you undermine me when it comes to their upbringing. When I tell Malcolm he can't have something, you go behind my back and give it to him. And I'm certain you would've had a hissy fit if someone did that to you when it came to Justin. Then there are times you act as if Zoe doesn't exist because you lavish all of your attention on her brother. I don't want my daughter growing up to resent Malcolm because you treat him as if he's the chosen one. I'm only a phone call away in case you need me."

She walked out, not seeing the tears filling the older woman's eyes because of those threatening to overflow from her own. Not only had she turned a page, but also a corner in her life—now she alone would be responsible for herself and her son and daughter.

Angela loaded the minivan with the bags, and without a backward glance, drove away from the home where she'd begun life as a new mother.

Chapter Seven

Lee waited at the door for Angela to emerge from the elevator. She'd called to let him know she'd been shown several properties and none met her specifications. He registered something in her voice when she said she'd gone back home to pick up more clothes. She hadn't mentioned that she'd had another confrontation with Miss Joyce, and he'd left it at that.

Lee felt the need more than before to take care of Angela. Looking for a place to call home while attempting to maintain a positive relationship with her children's grandmother was certain to take a toll on her emotionally.

He had been an eyewitness at an early age to the domestic upheaval between his mother and grandparents whenever they attempted to make her divorce his father because they felt he wasn't good enough for their daughter.

Lee had offered Angela safe haven at The Falls House when he actually wanted her to move in with him at the extended stay. However, suggesting she live with Viviana had worked well because his sister needed a positive person in her life after the recent debacle with her ex.

He smiled when Angela exited the elevator carrying a bag. Lee hadn't wanted her sleeping in the house alone—Viviana was attending a baby shower in Charleston for one of her high school classmates and staying over there after the event.

It was the first night of the Fourth of July three-day celebration and Angela had admitted she couldn't wait to eat hotdogs and cotton candy and ride the Ferris wheel. Reaching for her hand, he pulled her into the suite and closed the door. Cradling her face in his hands, he pressed a kiss to her forehead when he wanted to taste her mouth to discover if it was as sweet as it appeared.

"How are you?"

Angela dropped the bag and wrapped her arms around his waist. "Much better than I was several days ago."

He brushed several strands off her forehead that had escaped her loosely pinned bun. Lee smoothed out the slight worry lines between her eyes with his thumb. "The only thing on tonight's agenda is fun and more fun."

She smiled up at him. "I like the sound of that."

Lee scooped his keys off the dining table. "Let's roll, beautiful." During the drive to the fair he curbed the urge to ask Angela if she had given any thought to what he'd revealed to her at the Wolf Den. It wasn't as if she didn't know how he felt about her and now the ball was in her court to accept or reject his offer to take their friendship to another level.

The upside was they'd always gotten along and it probably was because they'd never been intimately involved with each other, unlike her and Justin, who at times appeared to have had a love-hate relationship. They appeared so much in love and then without warning they did not speak for several weeks, and then repeated the cycle so often that Lee wondered why they dated.

After seeing his parents' fractured marriage, he'd become very cynical when it came to affairs of the heart. The woman he'd been dating before he'd applied to Ranger School had unceremoniously announced she was engaged to someone else and that she'd only slept with him because she'd enjoyed the sex. He'd known men who used women for sex, and unknowingly the roles were reversed when he'd become an unsuspecting target.

Lee had no intention of making love with Angela until she made the first overture. He had waited fifteen years to make his feelings known, and he was willing to wait many more years to fulfill the promise he'd made to take care of her.

"Were you serious about wanting to date me?"

Angela's query broke into his thoughts. "Very serious," he said, as he stared out the windshield.

"Why?"

He gave her a quick glance. "Do you really have to ask me why? I've already told you how I feel about you."

"You talked about making a promise to Justin, but to me that doesn't translate into our having a relationship."

Lee counted slowly to ten. "Would it make a difference to you if I said that I'm in love with you? When Justin asked me to be the best man at your wedding my first reaction was to turn him down. But I didn't because I was given the chance to see you once more before you took your vows."

A ragged sigh echoed inside the vehicle. "Why didn't you say something?"

"Why would I, Angela? I didn't want you to think that perhaps you were marrying the wrong man."

"I didn't marry the wrong man because I truly did love Justin."

"I know you did," Lee said in a quiet voice.

Angela sighed again. "Do you think it's possible for me to love two men in one lifetime?"

"I can't answer that for you. There's only way to find out."

Angela's eyelids fluttered wildly. "I need time to process all of this because it's coming at me much too fast."

Lee chuckled. "Take all the time you need. I'm not going anywhere."

Angela saw the colorful lights from the various rides even before they entered the parking area where the carnival had been set up. Deputies from the sheriff's department were efficiently directing long lines of continuous traffic. It was reported that people came from as far away as the state capital to attend the three-day, two-night celebration. There were signs warning fairgoers not to bring handguns into the fair or they would be confiscated and returned only pending an appointment, and with the proper identification.

Lee helped Angela out of the jeep and sniffed the air like a large cat. "Smell that?"

She wrinkled her nose. "It smells like popcorn."

He smiled. "It's corn on the cob."

Angela slipped her hand in his. "Are we going to ride first or eat?"

Lee glanced up at a ride where riders were screaming at the top of their lungs as the baskets in which they were riding swung back and forth before rotating at crazy speeds. "Which one do you want to go on first?"

"I only ride the Ferris wheel."

He gave her an incredulous look. "You're kidding."

"No, I'm not."

"What about the roller coaster?" he asked.

Angela shook her head. "It's too scary fast."

Lee released her hand, curved his arm around her waist and pulled her against his side. "You can close your eyes while I hold you tight."

There came a beat. "Okay. I'll try it just once."

He pressed his mouth to her temple. "That's my girl." Lee led Angela to the ticket booth and purchased ten tickets.

"How many rides do you intend to go on?" she asked.

"We'll start with two and if you don't wimp out on me we can try a few others."

She gave him a sassy smile. "I just happen not to be a thrill seeker, unlike you who probably got a high from Special Forces HALO jumps."

Lee gave her a puzzled look. "How do you know about high-altitude military parachuting?"

"It was months after Justin's funeral that I recalled the reason why you'd lost so much weight and went online to look up the requirements for becoming Special Forces, and read about free-fall parachute jumps."

Lee wanted to tell Angela she was right. He'd earned a Master Military Freefall Parachutist Badge with three bronze combat stars centered on the dagger for five or more combat jumps. He'd stored his ranger tab and various medals in a felt-lined case along with a set of fatigues and a dress uniform in a plastic under-the-bed container.

He squeezed her fingers. "Now it's time to show me what you're made of."

"I'm no punk, Lee."

"We'll see."

Angela had overcome her fear of heights at the age of ten when she ventured to ride the Ferris wheel sitting between her mother and father. Her dad had reassured her he wouldn't let anything happen to her, because she was his precious princess. The butterflies in her belly had vanished once the car moved slowly upward, and when the wheel had made a full revolution she was hooked. Malcolm and Zoe were still too young to ride the wheel, but she planned to introduce them to her favorite ride once they reached the height requirement. Their car was suspended at the top of the wheel when the operator stopped it to load more riders.

"It's amazing how far we can see sitting up here," she said in awe. With a full moon and star-littered sky, the views from the ride were spectacular.

"You're right."

Angela shifted her gaze from the sky to Lee's profile. There was a longing in the two words that had garnered her attention, and she wondered whether he would have been been involved in some maneuver or combat mission on the other side of the globe if he hadn't come back to Wickham Falls, or if he and his team would be on high alert when seeking out an unseen or unidentified insurgent.

She'd given him furtive looks during his homecoming celebration at the Wolf Den, not recognizing the Leland she'd come to know in high school. He was more animated than she had ever seen him and realized it had to do with sharing a bond with those who had served. There were some men who lived for sporting events and others to collect cars, but for Lee it was the military. As a US Army Ranger he'd become a part of a brotherhood of men who did not judge him on his family history or his father's shortcomings, and Angela knew acceptance was something he'd sought all his life.

Angela had watched him eating by himself in the high school cafeteria until she told Justin that she was going to sit with him. She knew she'd shocked Lee when he stared at her with a pair of large blue-gray eyes that lacked warmth. She introduced herself and she had to wait a full minute before he told her his name and resumed eating. Justin joined them and they ate in silence until the bell rang. The following day Angela sat at Lee's table before his arrival and he thanked her and then apologized if he'd appeared rude, because he had not expected anyone to befriend him. What had begun as an awkward meeting had segued into an unbreakable bond that had continued to date.

Angela looped her arm through Lee's and rested her head on his shoulder. Justin had rarely defended her when she told him she'd overheard his mother's disparaging remarks about her, and the flipside was she always took his side whenever he complained about Joyce attempting to control his life. Rather than put down her mother-in-law, Lee had suggested she claim her own autonomy and independence. The wheel started up again and she closed her eyes. The feeling of weightlessness and the whisper of a warm breeze feathering over her exposed skin proved therapeutic for Angela. She didn't feel as confident as she had on the Ferris wheel when the operator fastened and locked the safety bar on the car of the roller coaster.

Lee grasped Angela's hand tightly. "Don't worry, babe. It's going to be fun."

"Because you say so?"

He laughed. "Because I know so. You'll see once it starts moving." The words were barely off his tongue when the cars began rolling along the track, quickly accelerating until it reached speeds exceeding sixty miles an hour. Angela had buried her face against his chest and screamed. His free hand cradled the back of her head as the ride slowed up a steep incline before hurtling down to a dip that continued into a loop, momentarily snatching the breath from his lungs. Angela was right. He was a thrill-seeking junkie. Speed and heights had become his drugs of choice.

The fifty-year-old Fourth of July fair had evolved from one day to two, and finally three, after the town council ruled that all businesses closed on the Fourth so employees can celebrate the holiday with their families. The next two days would also be town holidays with a fair-like carnival with rides, games and bake-offs, with business owners offering deep discounts to sell off inventory before the next season.

This was only the second time Lee had celebrated the holiday with the residents of The Falls. The first had been following his high school graduation and weeks before he signed his enlistment documents.

Holding Angela, feeling her warmth and inhaling the sensual fragrance of the perfume on her exposed skin had become an aphrodisiac. Everything about her—her face, body and voice—pulled him into a web of longing from which he did not want to escape. The instant she came over and sat across from him at the table in the school cafeteria he'd found himself mesmerized. So much so that he'd found himself unable to say more than his name. Angela was like a fairy-tale princess come to life, and once he had become more familiar with her he realized it wasn't just her natural beauty that held him spellbound whenever they were together, but also her willingness to form a friendship without expecting anything in return.

Lee later discovered he and Angela shared a common bond: alienation. The kids avoided him because of the stories about his unscrupulous ancestors who'd cheated and abused the men who'd worked in their mines, and the girls rejected Angela because she had made a name for herself as a successful teenage model. By age sixteen, her face had graced the covers of teen magazines, and during the school summer recess she traveled with her mother to Paris, Milan and Rome to model the upcoming lines of well-known designers.

She left the world of high-fashion modeling to become a wife, unaware it would be short-lived. Angela was the exemplary military widow when Lee sat next to her at Justin's funeral, holding one hand while her other rested on her rounded belly. Not once had she displayed grief during the service or when she was given the folded flag that had covered Justin's casket. It pained Lee to see her grieving inwardly and he was unable to offer the comfort he knew she needed from him as a friend. He hadn't wanted to be a friend but a husband to her and a father to her children yet to be born.

Lee knew he had wasted time by not keeping in touch with Angela, but that was going to change now that he was back in Wickham Falls. He had lost her once and he swore it would not happen again.

The ride ended and Angela's head popped up. Her eyes were shimmering with excitement. "Let's do it again."

He stared at her in disbelief. The wind had whipped her hair around her face. "You're kidding, aren't you?"

"No. That was incredible."

Throwing back his head, Lee laughed until his sides hurt. "You're unbelievable. Now who's the adrenaline junkie?" Reaching into the pocket of his jeans, he gave the ride operator two more tickets.

During their second ride Angela didn't hide her face in his chest but raised her arms above her head like many of the other riders did when the car sped up for a rapid decline. Her willingness to ride the roller coaster again told Lee that Angela was a risk-taker and that she was open to try something at least once.

The fairground was teeming with teenagers, mothers and fathers with their children, and people he recognized from Mineral Springs. For years there had been a fierce football rivalry between The Falls and The Springs.

Although Lee tended to eat healthy he could not resist the allure of carnival food. He ordered a sub with sausage, peppers and onions, while Angela indulged herself with a hotdog with mustard and grilled onions.

"Remind me not to kiss you before I brush my teeth," she teased.

Lee nodded because he didn't have a comeback. He'd kissed Angela but never on the lips. That was a line he did not want to cross unless she gave him permission. Hopefully it would happen sooner than later. They finished eating their sandwiches and washed it down with mugs of sweet tea.

Placing his arm around her waist, he led her over to the section where vendors had set up stalls with stuffed animals as prizes. He stopped at one where there were prizes for hitting moving ducks with an air rifle. "What kind of toys do your children like?" he asked Angela.

She studied the prizes. "Malcolm likes penguins and Zoe is partial to sock monkeys."

Lee placed a bill on the counter. "I'll buy three games." The vendor handed him the rifle and his change, and then pressed a lever. Lee raised the rifle and one by one in rapid succession he hit all ten ducks.

Angela stared in awe at Lee's sharpshooting skill as he knocked over every moving target. A small crowd had gathered to watch him and a smattering of applause broke out when he set down the rifle. The vendor picked up an extension pole and took down a penguin, a sock monkey and a white bear with a big red heart on its chest.

A middle-aged man with a long, gray ponytail

slapped Lee on the back. "Son, where did you learn to shoot like that?"

"Uncle Sam's Army."

The older man narrowed his eyes. "You Special Forces?"

Lee nodded. "Ranger."

"Well, it looks as if we have something in common. I was a Green Beret. Spent three years in Nam before I received a medical discharge after shrapnel tore through my left leg. The doctors wanted to amputate because it'd become infected. I told that SOB if he cut off my leg I was going to come back and gut him like a pig. He must have believed me because he ordered massive doses of antibiotics and three months later I walked out of the VA hospital with the legs I came into the world with."

Angela walked away to give the two men a modicum of privacy to compare war stories. She studied Lee as if it were her first time looking at him, and found him so primitively sensual, with his black hair floating around his face when not secured in a bun. Then there was the intensity in his eyes that had the power to not allow her to look away. His tawny complexion and seemingly balanced features that were the result of his mixed race ancestry made him a breathtakingly beautiful man.

A hint of a smile tilted the corners of her mouth when she wondered how had she gotten so lucky to have not one but two men in her life to love? Even though she did not want to admit it to herself, Angela knew Lee had always held a special place in her heart. Whenever her life was in crisis he was the one she'd reached out to: the spats she had with Justin in high school, her husband's death and now the confrontations with her mother-in-law. Lee had always come through offering support while not being judgmental. It had taken Lee fifteen years to admit to wanting more than friendship and he now he was offering her a second chance at love. He turned to look at her at the same time her smile grew wider.

He closed the distance between them and handed her the bear. "What are you smiling about?"

"I've just made a decision."

His black eyebrows lifted. "What about?"

"About us dating."

A beat passed. "What about us dating?"

"I'm ready to do it."

Leaning closer, Lee brushed a light kiss over her parted lips. "Thank you."

"Do you always kiss a girl on the first date?" she teased.

"Only if she lets me." He pressed a kiss to her ear. "One of these days I'm going to show you just how much I love you."

Angela did not have to be clairvoyant to know he was talking about making love with her. Passion had become as foreign to her as her past life as a model. It was a part of her past. She knew Lee wanted to make love to her and she wanted him to. After all, she was thirty, widowed and a mother of two who hadn't had sex since becoming pregnant. She was six weeks pregnant when Justin received orders that he was to be deployed, and he feared making love to her until she completed her first trimester, unaware he would never get the opportunity to sleep with his wife again.

"It's been a long time for me, Lee."

He angled his head. "I know that. I promise not to touch you until you're ready."

"What if I'm never ready?"

Lee lowered his eyes. "There are ways a man can release his sexual frustration."

Going on tiptoe, Angela kissed his cheek. "Are you blushing, Leland Remington?"

"No!"

"Someone is protesting too much." She looped her arms through his. "You can let me know when you need a sexual release and I'll see what I can do about it."

"Hot damn! I've got myself a saucy wench!"

"One of these days I'll show you a real saucy wench and I'm willing to bet you won't be able to handle her."

Lee leaned back slightly. "Are you challenging me? Because you know how much I love a challenge."

"Yes, sweet prince. It's a challenge."

Lee laughed so loud that people near them turned around. Angela tugged on his arm. "Let's go before folks think there's something wrong with you."

He stared at her, his blue-gray eyes holding her captive. "The only thing that's wrong is that I finally had to admit my feelings for you go beyond friendship."

Lee's passionate pronouncement stayed with Angela long after they'd left the fair. She spoke in monosyllables during the drive, and once they returned to his suite, she retreated to the bathroom to shower. When she emerged it was to close the bedroom door. The boldness she had exhibited had dissipated like hot water on a heated griddle.

Lee had come back into her life with the force of a twister sweeping up everything in its path and it frightened her. He didn't mince words, saying exactly what he wanted or felt and that was something she had to get used to. The young man she'd known in high school had evolved into a man she recognized but did not know. And it was the mature, adult Leland who made her feel something she had forgotten: desire.

Reaching over, she turned off the bedside lamp and closed her eyes. Sleep was a long time coming and when she did finally fall asleep, it was to dream of a man making love to her. She woke with a start, her chest rising and falling heavily as she tried to ignore the throbbing between her thighs. Angela sat up and covered her mouth to stop the slight moans from escaping. She gasped when the door opened and a tall shadow appeared in the doorway.

"Are you all right?"

Heat suffused her face when she realized Lee must have heard her moaning. "Yes. I just had a nightmare," she lied smoothly.

"So you want company?"

"No! Yes," she said quickly, patting the mattress next to where she lay. Angela knew she had to stop lying, something she detested and always cautioned her children against. "It wasn't a nightmare but an erotic dream. I had a dream you were making love to me." There, it was out. Now he knew everything.

Lee walked into the room and got into bed next to her. "Move over, babe."

Angela exhaled an inaudible sigh when she realized Lee was wearing pajama pants. "I..."

"Go back to sleep," he said, interrupting her and turning his back. "I need sleep if I'm going to be alert for tomorrow's military challenge."

"But, Lee..."

"Please stop talking, Angela," he said, cutting her off again.

She lay down and turned her back to his. Her celibate body was screaming for physical release and the man sharing the bed had no intention of assuaging her. His soft snores reverberated in the room and minutes later Angela fell asleep, too. She did not wake until ribbons of sunlight filtered through the drapes and the smell of coffee wafted to her nose. The pillow where Lee had slept beside hers bore the imprint of his head. Throwing off the sheet and lightweight blanket she headed for the bathroom.

"Don't take too long, sleepyhead," Lee called out from the kitchen. "Breakfast will be on the table in about fifteen minutes."

She smiled. "Aye, aye, Sergeant Remington."

"Wrong branch, princess."

"My bad!" she drawled as she closed the bathroom door. Angela knew she could easily get used to living with Lee. She did not go as far as thinking of them living together as husband and wife, but it was definitely something for her to think about for the future.

Chapter Eight

Angela knew she would either be hoarse or lose her voice completely as she screamed for Lee's team, led by Aiden Gibson, when they competed against Giles Wainwright's team during the tug-of-war. The participants wore tees and shorts stamped with their respective branch of service. All wore gloves to protect their hands against the hemp rope and military-issued boots as footwear. Giles had selected former marines to fill out his team, leaving Aiden to pick up those from the other branches.

Viviana, who had returned from her overnight stay in Charleston, nearly deafened Angela when she screamed at the top of her lungs. "Nicole, show the boys how it's done!" After giving the Corps fifteen years, Nicole Campos had gone to law school, returned to The Falls and was now an associate with the local law firm.

The red bandanna tied to the middle of the rope

went back and forth over the chalk line without either side giving quarter. Biceps and triceps were visible as the combatants fought for superiority. The heat from the sun, which had emerged from behind puffy clouds, beat down mercilessly on those gathered in the field to watch what had become a battle of gladiators.

Angela spied Joyce standing off from the crowd, frowning. Her expression indicated her distaste for the display of physical prowess, and she wondered if anyone or anything other than her grandchildren made her happy. Whenever she was around Malcolm and Zoe she'd become the overindulgent grandmother.

The competition continued for ten more grueling minutes, and then, without warning, the teams released the rope and declared it a draw, much to the disappointment of the spectators. A five-minute break ensued before the next competition: bell ringing. It was a team effort again and this time Aiden's team was awarded a first-place ribbon. Only six signed up for the weight-lifting contest. It began with bench-pressing one-fifty, increasing each round by fifty pounds.

Angela managed to push her way to the front of the crowd and held her breath as a pregnant silence fell over the assembled when Aiden failed to powerlift five hundred pounds. The next contestant also failed. She closed her eyes for several seconds as Lee lay on the bench and slowly lifted the barbell until it was above his head. Although not as heavily muscled as his team leader, he was younger and in peak conditioning compared to the former navy SEAL. He managed three repetitions before resting the bar on its stand. Hoots and whistles rent the air as Lee bowed as if he were an actor taking curtain calls.

Angela did not have time to react when Lee lifted her effortlessly off her feet and held her over his head. The crowd cheered with more hoots and whistles as he spun her around and around. *He's gone and lost his mind*, she thought as her heart pumped wildly against her ribs. He stopped spinning and slowly set her on feet. Angela gripped his shirt to maintain her balance. "You're going to pay for that," she threatened.

"What, babe? No congratulations?"

"Congratulations, Lee," she said, breathlessly. Angela hadn't expected him to use her as a human pinwheel. She saw Joyce out of the corner of her eye, glaring at her as if she had suddenly grown a set of horns. Looping her arm through Lee's she steered him away from the crowd that had gathered to watch the competition. "I'm ready to go home now."

"Do you want to come back later?"

"No. I need to go back to The Falls House and iron my clothes for the workweek." Angela had one more day before her vacation ended and it was back to work.

Lee exhaled an audible sigh. "Will I see you tomorrow?"

"Of course. Tomorrow afternoon is the bake-off competition, and I'm curious to see if Miss Joyce will win again this year." Angela untangled their arms. "I'll drive back."

"Are you sure?"

"Of course I'm sure, Batman. Sit back and relax. You've earned it." She tapped a button on the jeep's remote device, unlocking the doors. Lee sat next to her and she waited for him to secure his seat belt before turning on the engine and shifting into gear.

* * *

Angela woke to the sound of rain pelting the windows of her bedroom in The Falls House. It had been an unusually dry spring and although the region needed the rain, she would've preferred if it held off for twenty-four hours. It was the last and final day of the Fourth of July fair, and she knew if it didn't slack up or stop by noon the rest of the holiday's festivities would be canceled. Turning over she picked up the television remote, tuned to the weather channel and read the crawl on the bottom of the screen. Meteorologists were predicting torrential rain with flooding in valleys and low-lying areas. Last year the Chamber of Commerce had canceled the entire fair due to inclement weather, and Angela felt they were fortunate this year to get in at least two of the three days.

Angela turned off the television and stared up at the ceiling. It had taken the span of one week for her life to change: her children were with their maternal grandparents in Los Angeles; she'd moved out of her mother-in-law's house and into a historic mansion; she'd taken the first step to finding a house, and her relationship and feelings for Lee were changing and deepening with every encounter.

She'd asked him for time when Angela knew more time was an excuse, a ploy to delay the inevitable. Since reuniting with Lee she'd asked herself why she always looked for or called him when things didn't go right in her life.

Angela did not want to use Lee. He deserved loyalty, honesty and above all, love. Smiling, she closed her eyes. And he made it so easy for her to love him.

Her cell phone vibrated and she opened her eyes and picked it up.

"How did you know I was thinking about you?"

Lee's chuckle caressed her ear. "That's because I have super powers and can send vibes through the airwaves."

"Please don't tell me you believe the hype about being a superhero."

"Of course. You heard the dudes call me Batman, and the Dark Knight is the most popular of all the comic book superheroes."

"How about the Black Panther?"

"I'm definitely not in his league. What's on your schedule today?"

Angela sat up and swung her legs over the side of the bed. "I need to put in a load of laundry, and I promised Viviana that I'd help her dust and vacuum."

"Did she tell you we plan to reopen as a bed-and-breakfast?"

"No. She told me she closed down the boarding-house because she wanted to restructure the business." Angela listened intently as Lee outlined the plan for the new business. Wickham Falls usually attracted tourists in the late spring and summer and in the fall for hunting season. "Do you have a projected opening date?"

"Nothing that's definitive because there's work that has to be done. We'll probably have to update the plumbing and electricity, and make it Wi-Fi-accessible."

Viviana had given her a tour of the mansion, and Angela had concluded the suites in the wing of the house designated for lodgers required more refurbishing than the family wing. Her favorite space was the solarium, where floor-to-ceiling French doors bathed the space in light for the profusion of potted plants, ferns and trees growing in cultivated abandon.

"I'm certain once it's restored the house will once again become a spectacular showplace."

"You're probably right."

"I know I'm right, Lee. I'm certain you'll have a ribbon-cutting ceremony and folks will line up just to take a tour of what was and will become again the grandest house in The Falls."

"Why does it sound as if you're auditioning for the position as tour guide for the B and B?" Lee teased.

Angela smiled. "Perhaps I am."

"You know that can be arranged."

"Sign me up."

"You're hired."

"Thanks. I'm going to ring off now. I'll call you during the week to bring you up to date if I have any success finding a house."

"Good luck. I wanted to ask you if don't have anything planned for next Friday or Saturday night. I'd like to take you to the movies. And before you say anything, yes, I'm asking you out on a date."

"I thought when we went to the fair together that it was a date."

"It wasn't what I'd call an actual date."

Angela was curious as to what Lee considered a real date. "I'll make certain not to schedule anything for Friday night."

"Good. Is there a movie you'd like to see?"

"I like anything with a lot of action."

Lee laughed. "I'll see what I can come up with."

"Talk to you later."

"Later, princess."

Angela ended the call, wondering what had possessed her to leave her table in the school cafeteria and sit with Lee after watching him for nearly two weeks, and whether they were destined for their lives to be inexorably entwined after fifteen years of friendship.

Angela had stopping questioning the whys in her life and decided to let events unfold naturally. And if fate deemed it, then Lee would become a part of her life and future with her children.

Angela unlocked the rear door to the medical office, disengaged the security system and locked the door behind her. As the office manager, she made it a point to get there earlier than the rest of the staff. She turned on the air-conditioning unit, flicked on lights and booted up the computer in the reception, before powering on the television in the waiting area.

Drs. Franklin and Hawkins had given her a lot more responsibility when they promoted her from receptionist to office manager. Natalia had married newly-elected sheriff Seth Collier on May 1 in an outdoor fairy-tale ceremony.

She scrolled through the scheduled appointments. There were fewer than expected, which she attributed to families going on vacation. May was their busy month, with parents filling out forms for summer camp and college students updating immunizations.

Angela walked into the break room and filled the single-brew coffee maker and electric kettle with water before taking an inventory of coffee pods and tea bags. Maintaining the office in order to keep it running without a hitch was like taking care of her personal household—if she had one. She made certain to replenish medical supplies and equipment and keep track of the smocks and lab coats for the staff. Angela had also taken over accounts receivable, payable and patient billing— duties Dr. Franklin performed after visiting hours. The elderly doctor, with nearly forty years of practicing medicine, had hinted that he was ready to hang up his stethoscope in another year or two and transfer the practice to Natalia.

Angela had always wanted to be a school guidance counselor, but that dream was temporarily deferred when her modeling career took off. It was delayed again when she married Justin and got pregnant. She hadn't told anyone, but once Zoe and Malcolm were enrolled in school, she planned to apply to the University of Charleston at Beckley for a degree in Elementary Studies and Child Development.

The bell echoed throughout the office and she walked to the front door. Smiling, she unlocked it for the receptionist. "Good morning."

Maylis Roston, an empty nester who'd decided to reenter the workforce after raising her two sons, returned her smile. "Good morning to you, too. How was your vacation?"

"It was very nice." Angela did not want to tell Maylis that she didn't spend all of her two weeks in Florida.

"You took out your braids."

"Yes. But only for the summer."

Maylis ran a hand over her cropped hair. "I decided the day I turned forty I didn't want to bother sitting under a dryer or have some stylist burn my scalp when blow-drying my hair. I go to the barber every four weeks and they give me a buzz cut."

"You're lucky because you have the face for short hair."

"I'd wear it short even if I didn't have the face. I said if it's good enough for Judi Dench, then it's good enough for Maylis Roston." Maylis liked to mention the award-winning actress's name because people would remark how much Maylis resembled her. "I'm going to get some coffee before anyone gets here."

"I didn't check the refrigerator to see if there's milk," Angela said to her retreating back. "If you need some then let me know and I'll stop at the supermarket." It was her first day back and she had to go through the inventory of every item in the office to ascertain what was on hand and what needed to be replenished.

The back door chimed and a minute later Natalia walked into the reception area. When she'd returned from her Caribbean honeymoon her face was a rich mahogany-brown from the tropical sun. The petite former ER physician had left her position with a Philadelphia trauma center to move to Wickham Falls because she was experiencing burnout. She had let her hair grow, chemically relaxed it and had affected a sleek, sophisticated style.

"How was your vacation?"

"It was nice." Angela knew she would be asked the same question by everyone at the office. "I only spent a week in Florida because my parents took my kids to LA to visit my brother." She'd decided to tell Natalia the circumstances of her return to The Falls because she was certain her husband had seen her at the Wolf Den, and then during the military challenge.

"Seth told me he saw you at the Wolf Den. He wanted me to come with him, but I had to make a couple of house calls, so I decided to pass. He claims everyone had a good time welcoming a local boy home."

"Leland Remington and I were friends in high school. He was also a pallbearer at my husband's funeral."

Natalia shook her head. "I don't know why I keep forgetting that you're a widow. Maybe it's because you still wear your wedding rings."

Angela glanced at her left hand. She'd asked herself over and over why she didn't take off her rings and the answer was she didn't know. Perhaps, besides her children, it was her only link to Justin. Or maybe she did not want to explain to people that she had two babies and no husband.

"I'm so used to wearing them that I forget to take them off."

"The only time I wear my wedding band is on the weekend or when Seth and I go out together." Natalia glanced at the wall clock. "Henry's not coming in today, so it's just me."

"Is he all right?" Angela asked.

"He called me last night and said he needed a mental health day, so I told him I would cover his patients."

"Does Maylis know to give you his patients?"

"She should because I sent her an email."

"I'll double-check with her to make sure she knows." Angela and Natalia had devised a system where they electronically transferred the patient records to the respective doctor's computer to review before seeing them. "Fortunately we don't have too many scheduled for today."

Natalia nodded. "Hopefully we'll be able to close up on time."

"I'm going to keep my fingers crossed we don't get walk-ins."

* * *

The week went by quickly for Angela. The office opened and closed on time, and there was only one emergency. A little boy had fallen and cut the palm of his hand, and Dr. Franklin closed the cut with a few sutures before administering a tetanus shot.

Milly Riley showed Angela two more properties. They were an improvement over the others but still required updates to the kitchen and bathroom, and extensive landscaping. She had reached the point where she felt she would never find a house she liked. The owners who'd bought her parents' house had expanded the rear for entertaining and had no intention of selling it back to her.

Viviana came to her bedroom the night before and revealed she'd met with her lawyer who was in the process of forming a new corporation. She and Lee had contacted an engineer to inspect the property to ascertain it was structurally sound before restoring the house to its former state. Her disclosure made Angela even more anxious to find a place to live before her children returned home.

On Friday, her phone's ringtone indicated a text message. It was Lee and he was waiting outside the house for her. When she asked Viviana why her brother had elected to check in at the extended stay when he had a home, she mumbled something about Lee having beef with their father.

She picked her shawl and cross-body off the chair and walked out of the bedroom. Angela didn't want to get too involved with the Remington family feud when she still hadn't resolved her own issues with Justin's mother.

Lee was leaning against the bumper of the jeep when she emerged from the house. He stood straight and smiled. It was apparent he was glad to see her, and she him. He was casually dressed in a pair of tan slacks, an untucked white shirt and cognac-colored oxfords. He'd cut his hair and brushed the thick waves off his forehead.

"You look very handsome."

Lee kissed her cheek. "Thank you. I thought I'd clean up a bit for our first official date."

"I must say you clean up nicely."

He cupped her elbow and led her around to the SUV's passenger side. "I have to step up my game in order to keep up with you."

Angela waited until he'd sat next to her and said, "There's nothing to keep up with."

Lee draped his arm over the back of her seat. "You're not some girl from a small town boasting two stop lights and a population that's struggling to stay above four thousand. You've experienced places and things people in The Falls never get to see or do in their lifetime. By the time you were sixteen you'd traveled to major European cities folks here only see in movies or on television. And once you graduated you lived abroad for years like an ex-pat. I'm talking about your maturity and your sophistication that is so much a part of you that you take it for granted. I may be what people think of as an elite soldier, but that's all I am. I eat, sleep and breathe military as if my next breath depended on my survival."

Angela touched his clean-shaven jaw. "You're wrong, Lee. You're more than just a soldier. You're a brother, a son, and you are loyal and selfless almost to a fault.

And before we graduated you swore you would never come back to The Falls to live, but you have. Viviana told me that you put in for a discharge to come back and help her with her business." She pressed her mouth to his. "Self-deprecation doesn't suit you."

"I guess you told me."

Angela nodded. "Yes, I did."

"I'd like to ask you one thing before we leave."

"What's that."

"May I kiss you?"

She stared into eyes that appeared more blue than gray. "Yes, you may."

Lee's moist breath feathered over her mouth before he kissed her with a tenderness she hadn't thought possible. It was as if she were fragile crystal and he feared she would break if he applied too much pressure. The kiss ended in seconds, leaving her mouth on fire and wanting more. So much more.

"That was very nice for the first course."

"Oh! Now I'm a meal?" she said, teasingly.

"No. You're an entire smorgasbord, and one of these days I'm going to sample every course from your head to your toes and not stop until I've had dessert and an aperitif."

Pinpoints of heat stung her face with his passionate description of lovemaking. Angela wanted to beg him to make love to her but a silent voice said no. She was more than aware that once they made love neither of them or their lives would ever be the same. She stared out the side window as Lee maneuvered the circular driveway.

"What movie are we going to see?"

"You said you wanted action and I found a little

movie house outside of Beckley showing films that are at least six months old. Did you ever see *Sicario*?"

Angela's pensive mood changed as she became more animated. Her smile was dazzling. "Yes. Even though it was a tad violent, I still loved it."

"Only a tad, princess? It was very violent."

"That's because of the storyline. I gave it a pass because Benicio Del Toro is my favorite actor."

"Well, you're about to see your favorite actor again in the sequel: *Sicario: Day of the Soldado*."

"Have you seen it?"

Lee gave her a quick glance. "But of course."

"And you don't mind seeing it again?"

"Anytime someone makes a movie about good guys and villains fighting I'm all in."

"My designated movies are PG until the kids are older, then I'll graduate to PG-13."

"You can always get a babysitter to watch the kids whenever you have a date night."

"Justin and I never had what you would consider a normal relationship. He was in college while I was modeling, and even when I came back we rarely got together because he had gone to medical school. Then he dropped out and enlisted and we still didn't get to see that much of each other." A pregnant silence filled the vehicle, swelling until it became deafening. Angela realized Lee rarely had a comeback whenever she mentioned her late husband's name. "Does it bother you when I talk about Justin?"

"Why should it bother me?" He'd answered her question with one of his own. "Justin was my friend, your husband and the father of your children."

"And he wasn't perfect."

Lee accelerated into the flow of interstate traffic. "None of us are perfect, Angie. We all have flaws."

"I know, but Justin had flaws that I chose to overlook. I forgave him for a lot of things. When I used to come to you whenever Justin and I stopped speaking it was because…"

"No, babe," he interrupted, shaking his head. "I didn't want to know why you and Justin broke up back in the day and I still don't want to know the details now. We're different people than we were in high school. And that means I've moved on, Angela."

"And I need to move on, too, beginning with our first date night."

Lee's smile was dazzling. "That's my girl. Do you want to eat before or after the movie?"

"After."

Lee sat across the table from Angela in a tiny restaurant that specialized in authentic Asian-fusion cuisine. He'd ordered tom yum goong, spicy and sour Thai soup with shrimp, lemongrass and mushrooms, and a Chinese style entrée shrimp and broccoli with basil fried rice. Angela had selected spring rolls with Thai sweet and sour sauce, and chicken pad Thai for her entrée.

Over dinner they became reviewers, dissecting every scene in the film. "Did you enjoy the sequel more than the original?" he asked her.

Angela rested her elbow on the cloth-covered table and cupped her chin on her hand. "It's a toss-up. I probably need to see them again back-to-back to make an unbiased decision."

"Would it help if I buy the DVDs and plan for a *Sicario* marathon?"

She smiled. "That'll work. By the way, how did you find this place? The food is phenomenal."

A mysterious smile played at the corners of Lee's mouth. "I googled restaurants in the area and it came up with a number of excellent reviews."

"Oh."

Sitting back on his chair, Lee couldn't stop laughing at how her expressive face changed, becoming somber. "I'm sorry to disappoint you, but this is my first time eating here."

"You've just become the designated restaurant chooser. You select the restaurant and I'll just show up."

"You're giving me a lot of responsibility."

"What's the matter, sport? You don't trust your instincts?"

"The only thing I trust is my own cooking."

"That's because you're an incredible cook."

Lee angled his head. "I can't take the credit. Aunt Babs taught me well."

"Remember me inviting myself to your house for study group and hanging around so your aunt would invite me to stay for supper?"

"Your mama is no slouch in the kitchen," Lee countered. "Her oxtails and short ribs were to die for."

Angela traced the design on the handle of her knife with a finger. "I have a binder filled with my mother and grandmother's favorite recipes. Once I get my own kitchen I'm going to make every one of them."

Lee reached across the table and caught her hand. "I don't want you stressing out because you can't find a house. I am serious when I say you can stay at The Falls House for as long as it takes for you to move into your new home."

Her head popped up. "It's not adding up. You invite me to stay in a house where you refuse to live."

He released her hand. "It's not as simple as that."

"Talk to me, Lee. Tell me why I'm sleeping in your house while you sleep in a converted motel off the interstate."

Lee stared at the wooden carving on the opposite wall. He knew he owed it to Angela to reveal the bitter enmity between him and his father because he loved her and wanted her in his life. "I'd planned to stay but Vivi didn't tell me that Emory had come back."

"You call your father Emory?"

"It's been a long time since I'd called him Dad."

It was Angela's turn to cover his hand with hers. "You can tell me it's none of my business but if we're going to be together then I need to know about why you're estranged from your father."

If we're going to be together. Lee stared at Angela, complete surprise freezing his features with her prediction of their possibly sharing a future. He nodded. "You have every right to know. Let me settle the check and I'll tell you everything on the drive back to The Falls."

Chapter Nine

Angela listened without saying a word as Lee revealed the circumstances surrounding his parents' marriage.

Annette Wolfe met Emory Remington in college where she was an education major and he a part-time art student. She hadn't told her parents she was dating a man of African and Native-American ancestry until she found herself pregnant. Both of them dropped out, married, and Annette convinced Emory to come with her to Wickham Falls so he could meet her family.

"All hell broke loose, and my grandmother took to her bed, while my grandfather threatened to disinherit his youngest daughter because he'd expected her to marry the son of a prominent Virginia politician."

"She never told Emory she was engaged?"

"No, because it was an arranged marriage. Emory refused to live in the same house as his in-laws and rented a second-floor apartment in a row house on Pike

Road. He issued Annette an ultimatum: she could live with him or stay with her parents. In the end she opted to live with her husband. Money was tight and Emory used his artistic talent when he found a job as a sign painter. Mom got pregnant, but lost the baby when she was four months along after she slipped and fell down a flight of stairs.

"Meanwhile Emory enlisted in the Marines and earned more than what he'd made working for the sign company. Mom got pregnant again and this time she carried to term and delivered me. Two years later she had Viviana."

"Was your dad still in the military?"

"Yes. He deployed to Kuwait during Desert Storm, where he was wounded and eventually medically discharged. He was prescribed powerful pain killers, which eventually led to his drug addiction. I was only six, but I can remember my mother pleading with him to go into treatment or she was going to divorce him. He'd get clean for a few months, then he would relapse. During this time my grandmother had passed away and Grandpa was practically bedridden after a series of heart attacks. That's when Mom decided to move back to The Falls House.

"She ran the household, took care of me and Vivi, and looked after her father. Emory would be there and then without warning he would disappear for months. Whenever I asked him where he was going and when he was coming back he'd mumble, *'I don't know.'* And whenever I asked my mother if my father was coming back she would say, *'Hopefully soon.'* What I did not or could not understand as I grew older was why my mother took her marriage vows seriously. She had stuck by her husband in sickness and in death, and she'd died still loving and believing in him.

"Mom enrolled me and Vivi in the private school where generations of Wolfes had been educated. We lived on campus during the week and came home on weekends. Everything changed when Mom started falling. At first she attributed it to clumsiness and then her sister urged her to see a doctor. That's when they discovered she had an inoperable brain tumor. Aunt Babs sold her DC condo, married her boyfriend and moved back to West Virginia to take care of her terminally ill sister and invalid father. Grandpa died in his sleep several days before celebrating his seventy-second birthday. His last will and testament bequeathed the house to Mom and divided between his daughters his shares of mineral rights on large tracts of land with natural gas.

"My mother, blatantly aware of her own mortality, drew up a will and left the house and remaining twelve acres on which it sat to me and Viviana. We were also equal recipients of her life insurance. The terms of the policy designated her older sister Barbara Wolfe-McCarthy as executor and legal guardian for her children until their eighteenth birthdays. The only time I saw my father cry was when he showed up out of the blue and discovered his wife was dying. She admitted she still loved him and would with her last breath."

Angela swallowed the lump in her throat as she struggled not to become emotional. "Where was he living?"

"There were rumors that he was living in a flophouse across the tracks and I'd overheard my aunt tell my mother that the sheriff had locked him up after he was found him sleeping off a high in someone's back-yard. Emory was arrested again, this time for robbing a gas station at gunpoint. He claimed his dealer had threatened to kill him if he didn't pay him for drugs he'd stolen from him. Emory was tried, convicted and sentenced to five years in the state prison for armed robbery. The next and last time I saw him was at my mother's funeral. Two marshals had escorted him into the church wearing handcuffs and shackles. I was nine years old and that was the last image I had of my father until a couple of weeks ago."

"What did you say to him?"

"Nothing. I was so angry with Vivi because she could've warned me that he was staying with her."

"Viviana told me he'd gone to Philly for a few weeks and would let her know when he was coming back."

"That has to be a first."

"What is?"

"His telling someone of his comings and goings."

"People do change, Lee."

"Some do and some don't."

Angela registered the hardness in Lee's voice. "You don't believe your father can change?"

"It has nothing to do with what I believe, Angela. It's been twenty-one years since I last saw the man and not once in all of that time has he attempted to reach out to me. He may have loved his wife but not more than he craved his drugs and alcohol."

"Maybe one of these days you can find it in your heart to forgive him."

Lee took his eyes off the road for a millisecond. "Let it go, Angela."

Her nerves tensed as she glared at him. "Do you

intend to shut me down every time I say something you don't want to hear? Either we discuss things like mature adults or not talk at all. I had enough of that with Justin."

"Why do you always compare me to Justin?"

Angela clenched her hands until her nails bit into her palms. "I won't unless you do something that reminds me of things that annoyed me about him."

The inside of the jeep would've been as silent as a tomb if not for the audible sound of Lee's breathing as he struggled to not lose his temper. He'd stripped himself bare when he revealed to Angela things he'd only admitted to the army psychiatrist. Talking about his mother's funeral and seeing his father shackled had brought back images it had taken him years to forget. And Angela had suggested he forgive his father, when it was Emory who should be the one to ask for forgiveness for deserting his wife and children when they needed him most.

His mother had died with Emory's name on her lips, and he had grown up without a father. Emory should've been there when it came time to talk to him about sex and what it took to grow up to become an honorable man. And where was he for Viviana? Fathers were supposed to love and protect their daughters. Lee knew he didn't have to be a genius to know his sister was looking for a man to replace the father who was never there for her.

Angela didn't know what it was to grow up without her parents. He'd lost both parents at an early age—his mother to a terminal disease and his father to illegal substances and eventually prison.

He chose his words carefully. "Tell me now if I'm going to have to compete with a dead man and if I am then I'll walk away and never bother you again."

"Are you looking for an excuse to quit me, Leland Wolfe Remington?"

He laughed in spite of the seriousness of their conversation. "Why did you have to go and say my entire government name?"

"Because I'm angry as hell, Leland. You tell me you love me and now you're ready to cut and run."

"Rangers don't cut and run."

"Right now you're not a ranger. You're someone I'm falling in love with and need in my life. Don't play with my feelings or I'll make you sorry you ever met me."

"What are you going to do? Body slam me?"

"Now you've got jokes? You know I can't lift you."

"That's because I probably weigh twice as much as you do and that means I can bench press you with one arm."

"Showing off?"

He winked at her. "Why not flaunt it when you've got it?" Lee sobered when he remembered what they were arguing about. "I meant it when I told you I love you and want you in my life."

Angela went still. "And I told you I needed time to think about it."

Lee decided to press the issue now that she'd admitted to falling in love with him. "How much more time do you want?"

"I...I don't know."

"Give me a timeframe, Angie. Next week? Next month?"

"The end of summer."

"Good. And you can stop looking for a house because we'll live at The Falls House."

"How long have you been concocting this scenario?"

"It's been a while."

"How long is a while, Lee?"

"It was probably a year after you buried Justin. The promises we had made to one another in high school kept nagging at me. I wanted to come back and see you but I was afraid you'd think of me as a creep looking to take advantage of your vulnerability."

"Why now, Lee?"

"I've seen and done things that remind me of my own mortality. It also made me aware of the fragility of human life. It's taken me this long to know I'm now mature enough to become a husband and father. And if we do decide to marry we don't have to wait to plan for children because I'll already have a son and daughter."

The passion in his voice when he mentioned having a son and daughter made Angela's breath catch in her chest. "Will you want more children?"

"Of course. There are five bedroom suites, and we're going to need a bunch of kids to fill up those rooms."

"You've gone and lost your mind if you think I'm going to have five children. And what about Viviana? Where will she live?"

"She's always said that she prefers living in the guesthouses because she likes her privacy."

"So it will just be us in the big house?"

"Yes. The B and B will be run out of a separate wing of the main house. Once the B and B is up and running Vivi will hire a staff of house and groundskeepers. Of course I'll help her, but she'll be the general manager."

* * *

A shiver of excitement eddied through Angela when she thought about how life as she knew it was going to change if she married Lee. Once the word got out she was going to become Mrs. Leland Wolfe Remington the gossips would have a field day talking about Emory's boy marrying his best friend's widow, and that Lee probably had always coveted his friend's wife.

Let them talk, she mused. Some said Justin would still be alive if she hadn't convinced him to drop out of medical school and join the military like Leland. A lie possibly perpetrated by Joyce and repeated by others. Church ladies whispered to one another if they saw the same man sit in her pew more than once.

Angela also had her share of would-be suitors who probably considered her as a good catch. None of them knew she wasn't interested in landing another husband; her entire existence revolved around taking care of her babies. Her three-year-olds were verbal, completely potty-trained and ready for all-day childcare. And her inquisitive son who wanted a daddy was going to get his wish once she and Lee married.

"If we do decide to marry, where do you want to hold the ceremony?" she said after a comfortable silence.

"Do you want another courthouse ceremony?"

Angela shook her head. "No." She wanted to tell Lee that it was too impersonal. "I'd like something simple and a little more traditional."

"What about The Falls House? If we hold it there, then we'll need to fast-track the repairs."

"Maybe we shouldn't set a date until everything's completed," Angela suggested.

Lee patted her knee. "I'll leave all of the planning

to you. Just let me know the date and the time and I'll show up."

Her smile mirrored the joy wrapping Angela in a cocoon of soaring peace. She had always loved Lee as her best friend, confidant and protector, which wasn't the same as being in love with him. Angela now knew there was something special about the boy who'd appeared unfazed by the alienation from many of the students at his new school.

"I'm going to ask Viviana to help with the planning."

"The two of you are certain to be a dynamic duo."

She smiled. "You think?"

Lee nodded. "I know."

Angela unlocked the door to the house that she could now think of as home, and then turned to face Lee. "Is this when I invite you in for coffee?"

"Yes, but not tonight. Go inside and lock the door before I do something I may come to regret."

Angela didn't know whether he was talking about making love to her, or crossing the threshold of the house where he'd experienced memories he still had not been able to exorcise. The night was one of looking back and planning forward. She knew it wasn't easy for Lee to talk about his parents, and she felt his pain as surely as if it was her own. He'd talked about his past and now they were planning for their future.

"Good night, Lee."

"Good night, Angela."

She walked into the house, then closed and locked the door behind her. Angela stood in the same spot for several minutes before she realized Viviana was standing there. The younger woman was dressed in a tank top and sweatpants.

"Did Lee and I wake you?"

Viviana ran her fingers through a mane of curly black hair, the style reminiscent of a younger Cher. "No. I was waiting for you to come home because I wanted you to let know I'll be away for a week. Some of my friends from college are gifting me with a seven-day cruise for my birthday."

"That's wonderful news!"

Viviana clasped her hands together. "It's been a while since I've been able to hang out with them because I couldn't leave the boardinghouse. But now there's nothing keeping me here until I get word that the contractor will begin working on the house."

"Have you told Lee?"

"Not yet. I wanted to tell you first, and I'm willing to bet he won't let you stay here alone. Even though Dad's not coming back until the end of July or the beginning of August I'm going to try and convince Lee to stay here with you."

"I really don't need him to babysit me." Angela decided it was it wasn't the right time to tell Viviana that she planned to marry her brother. "When are you leaving?"

"Not for another two weeks. Hopefully by that time we'll know the timeline for sprucing up this old house to get it ready to reopen as a bed-and-breakfast. I've been up working up on the plans for how I want the B and B. If you're not ready to turn in, then I'd like you to see what I've come up with."

"Give me a few minutes to change and wash my face, and I'll join you."

Viviana flashed a knowing smile. "How is it to date my brother?"

"It's okay."

"Just okay?"

Angela met her future sister's-in-law eyes. "It's really great."

"I told Lee that you married the wrong friend. But I suppose you had to marry Justin to get those adorable twins."

Angela sobered and became reflective. "You're right about that."

"When am I going to see your babies?"

She spoke to her mother several times a week and made certain to FaceTime her son and daughter as they competed with each other to see who could be the first tell her what they'd done or seen that day.

"My parents are planning to bring them back at the end of July. Mom and Dad will stay overnight and then head down to Daytona Beach to reopen their home and get ready for the new semester."

A wistful expression settled into Viviana's delicate features. "You're really blessed to have grown up with both parents. You know about my father. He definitely was a rolling stone—here today and gone tomorrow. I remember my mom sleeping all the time. She would either lie in bed or sit on a chair and always in the dark. She complained about the light hurting her eyes, and it wasn't until I was older that I realized she had a brain tumor. Even though I totally love my Aunt Babs, she still wasn't Mom. When I asked my aunt why she didn't have children she said me and Lee were her children and that was enough for her. I remember telling her that when I have my kids I'm going to hold them so tight they're going to beg me to let them go."

Angela heard the longing in Viviana's voice. "Children will definitely change you and your life—forever."

"Do you want more children, Angela?"

"I'd like at least one more," she said truthfully.

Viviana waved her hand. "I'm standing here running my mouth when you want to change. When you come down I'll be in the kitchen."

Angela sat at one of the two tables in the expansive kitchen, studying the contents of a folder Viviana, with the assistance of an interior decorator, had created to document what she wanted for her new business enterprise. The file also included before and after photographs of various suites with plans to replace bathtubs with two-person Jacuzzis. Wood-burning fireplaces would be converted to gas. All suites would have flat-screen televisions and Wi-Fi.

"I know it's going to be costly, but I want all of the beds to have Egyptian cotton monogrammed sheets."

Angela pointed to a photo of the dining room. "Do you plan to remove the wallpaper?"

"I'm still debating that. If I'm going to repaper the walls then I want more contemporary textured fabrics." Viviana paused. "I don't want to modernize the interiors too much because it'll lose the appeal of a late nineteenth-, early twentieth-century home."

"The exteriors look more antebellum South than Victorian," Angela remarked.

"That's because the wife of the original owner was from South Carolina. Her parents once owned a plantation before the Civil War. They were on the verge of disowning her because she married a Yankee. The upside was he was a very wealthy Yankee. Years later she brought her mother to live with her and when the older woman saw Wolfe House she felt as if she'd come home."

Angela wanted to ask Lee's sister if she was aware of history repeating itself when her grandfather threatened to disinherit her mother because she'd married a man they hadn't chosen for her. "Who told you this story?"

Viviana smiled. "No one. I read about it. There's a chest in one of the rooms on the third floor that is filled with correspondence to and from Wolfes going back to the Spanish-American War. If you want I can show them to you."

"I'd love to read them." She turned another cellophane-covered page. "I like the proposed changes to the drawing room."

"That's where I plan for lodgers to gather in the evening for tea cakes and cordials. Those who stay overnight will be served a gourmet buffet breakfast with freshly brewed cappuccino, eggs Benedict, bacon, ham, sausage, chicken and waffles, organic fruit, yogurt and a variety of breakfast cereals."

"Yummy!" Angela drawled.

"I agree. I already have a commitment from a guy willing to do the cooking. I asked him to put the word out that I'm looking for a baker."

"Have you considered Joyce Mitchell?" The question was off Angela's tongue before she could censor herself.

"Your mother-in-law?" Viviana questioned.

"Yes. She may have many faults, but baking is not

one of them. Remember she's won more bake-off prizes than anyone in Johnson County."

Viviana massaged her forehead with her fingers, appearing deep in thought. "You're right about that. I know you're on the outs with her, so I'll approach her about possibly providing some baked goods for the B and B."

It had been almost two weeks since Angela's last tense encounter with the woman. If Joyce was amenable to producing bake goods for the bed-and-breakfast it would give her an opportunity to focus on something other than her grandchildren.

She had recommended her mother-in-law because she was the best when it came to baking pies and cakes. "Even though we're not getting along, I'll broach the subject with her before you approach her with your proposal."

Viviana pressed her palms together in a prayerful gesture. "I hope she'll come through."

Angela turned another page and peered closely at the proposed change to one of the guesthouses. "Won't you have to raise the roof if you add a loft off the living room?"

Viviana leaned closer, her shoulder touching Angela's. She peered at the page and nodded. "That's what I want, but I'm not certain the architect will approve it. The loft will be large enough for a king-size bed. Both guesthouses have two bedrooms, and with the addition of the loft there will be more than enough space for a family of four."

"Have you thought of advertising one of the guesthouses as a rental apartment? That way you'd have guaranteed monthly income."

"Hey now! That's a good idea."

Angela spent the next forty-five minutes listening to Viviana outline what she wanted for her new business and how it would differ from the boardinghouse. The solarium, which had been off-limits to boarders would be available for B and B guests to relax before and after breakfast. She also wanted to build an outdoor kitchen with a bar, gas grill, pizza oven and a fire pit. "I have something to tell you before I turn in for the night."

Viviana stared, wide-eyed, and went completely still. "You're moving out?"

"No. I'm moving in. Permanently. Lee and I are thinking about getting married."

Viviana screamed as if she had been stabbed with a sharp object. "Really?"

Angela smiled. "Really. We won't set a date until the renovations to the house are completed."

"You plan to hold the ceremony here?"

"Yes. I need your help planning it. I want something small, intimate and most of all informal, with family and close friends."

"What about the reception? Do you want sit-down or buffet-style?"

"Buffet. And if we have nice weather, then it can be held outdoors under a tent."

Viviana hugged Angela so tight she feared being choked to death. "I can't believe I'm going to be an auntie." She loosened her hold on Angela's neck. "Anytime you need a babysitter, Auntie Vivi is available."

Reaching up, Angela managed to extricate herself. "I'm going to warn you in advance that Zoe and Malcolm can be double-trouble."

Viviana made a sucking sound with her tongue and

teeth. "I've been called the kid whisperer. Once they're around Auntie Vivi it's night-night."

Angela found Viviana's bubbly personality contagious. "If someone told me I was going to get the perfect sister, I would've called them a liar. Thank you for allowing me to become a part of your family."

"Girl, please. You're the one I should be thanking. You marrying my brother will definitely add some respectability to the Wolfes and Remingtons." She pointed to Angela's bare left hand. "Do you realize this is the first time since you married Justin that I've seen you without your rings?"

Angela stared at the third finger of her left hand. There was a lighter band of color where the sun hadn't darkened it. "I'm going to save them for Malcolm in case he wants to give them to his fiancée. The center stone in the engagement ring belonged to Justin's grandmother. I decided to take them off because I don't want to have a relationship with Lee with the shadow of Justin hovering over us. A part of Justin will be connected to us because of Malcolm and Zoe."

"Do you and Lee plan to have more children?"

"Lee mentioned having children but I'd like to wait until the twins are in the first grade. By that time Lee and I will be thirty-three and I'll still have another year or two if we decide to have another one."

"It you decide to have four, then it's the perfect number to fill up the bedrooms in the family wing. And even if I'm not married by that time I have no problem living in the guesthouse. I'll probably move into one of them once you guys are married. Newlyweds are entitled to their privacy. Not living under the same roof but on the same property will be a win-win for everyone."

Angela recalled Lee mentioning that Viviana preferred the guesthouse because she coveted her privacy. She stood. "I'm going to bed before I fall on my face. Night-night."

Viviana stood. "Good night, sis."

Angela waved, smiling, and walked across the kitchen to the back staircase. So much had happened in a matter of hours to impact her life that Angela knew she would have to replay the scenes like the frames of a film. She and Lee had had their first official date; he'd mentioned marriage and she was looking forward to the time when they would become husband and wife.

Her future sister-in-law had asked for her opinion on restoring the historic house which was to become Angela's new home with her husband and children.

And she had voluntarily removed the rings that represented a vow she had made to the man who'd fathered her children. Justin was gone but she knew he was smiling down on her because he knew his best friend was going to keep his promise to take care of his wife and children if anything happened to him.

Promises made were to be promises kept.

Chapter Ten

Angela placed her foot on the first step leading to the porch, staring behind the lenses of her sunglasses at Joyce glaring back at her. It had taken a week before she found the time to approach the woman. Each time she dialed her number to inform her she wanted to see her, it went directly to voice mail. It was apparent the woman was still fuming about her moving out. In the end she decided to come over and catch her off-guard.

"I'd like to talk to you about something."

Joyce's hands tightened on the arms of the rocker. "There's nothing you have to say I need to hear."

Angela took another step. "I think you do."

"I don't want to hear it unless it concerns my grand-children."

"It does. But I also want to talk to you about some-thing else. Please don't get up, Joyce," Angela ordered

sharply. "Just sit there and listen to what I have to say."
She must have gotten through to the older woman as
shock froze her features. "I know you don't like the
Wolfes or the Remingtons but Viviana would like for
you to go into business with her." Joyce sat straight.
That got your attention, didn't it? Angela thought as
she bit back a grin.

"What kind of business?"

She walked up on the porch and sat on a cushioned
chair facing Joyce. "She plans to reopen the house in
the fall as a bed-and-breakfast and she would like for
you to provide breakfast baked goods and tea cakes for
after-dinner gatherings. She wants to know if you're
open to talking to her about it."

Joyce averted her eyes. "Tell her I'm willing to listen to whatever she has to say." Angela hid a smile.
She knew the older woman would agree, because nothing pleased Joyce more than having people praise her
baking.

Joyce's expression changed as she closed her eyes for
several seconds. "I know I never told you before but if
you hadn't moved in with me after losing Justin I don't
know what I would have done."

"My moving here was something we both needed
at the time."

"What about now, Angela?"

Angela tensed up. "What about now?"

"You're living over in the big house with those people."

"Those people are going to be my family when I
eventually marry Leland. Yes," she reiterated when
Joyce looked as if she was going to pass out, "he asked

me to marry him and I said I would." She didn't tell
Joyce that Leland hadn't officially proposed and that
she had accepted. "Now Malcolm will get the daddy
he's been asking for." She held up a hand when Joyce
opened her mouth. "Please let me finish. You will always be my children's Grammie, and I promise to never
keep them from you. They love you and I know you
love them but I don't need yours or even my parents'
permission to marry. What I need is for you to be happy
for me and your grandchildren."

Joyce gave her a direct stare. "I know it hasn't been
easy for you living with me, and I'm sorry if I over-
stepped my role as a grandmother when interfering
with how you want to raise your children. I promise it
won't happen again."

A beat passed. Angela nodded. "I accept your apol-
ogy, and hopefully starting now we can put all of that
behind us. I'd like to extend an invitation that if you
want to come and spend time or even the night with
Malcolm and Zoe, the doors to The Falls House will
always be open to you."

Joyce shook her head and at the same time wagged a
finger at Angela. "Didn't I tell you that boy was sweet
on you?" she said smugly.

Angela lowered her eyes and smiled. "Yes, you did."

"I guess if you wait long enough you'll eventually
get what you've always wanted."

"I suppose it worked in Lee's case."

Joyce pointed at Angela's hand. "What did you do
with your rings?"

"I've put them away for Malcolm." This disclosure
seemed to please Joyce and she smiled. "Only Viviana, you and my parents know that I'm marrying Lee,

and I'd to keep it like that until we set a date. We plan to hold the ceremony and reception at The Falls House and I'd be honored if you'd come. I'm certain the twins will want their Grammie to see them dressed in their wedding finery."

Joyce grunted and averted her eyes. "I guess I can come."

"I can't have you guessing."

Joyce's head swung back "Okay. I'm coming. What about the cake?"

Angela bit her lower lip to keep from smiling. "What about it?" Although Joyce had never gone to pastry school she had a gift for creating elaborately decorated wedding cakes, some with edible flowers.

"Who's going to make your wedding cake?"

"I don't know yet."

"I'd like to volunteer to make it."

"I can't impose on you like that," Angela said in protest.

"It wouldn't be an imposition," Joyce countered. "And I have the perfect design in mind. I can make four checkerboard layers of carrot, red velvet, white and devil's food cake. The top layer will be plain yellow cake. I can also make individual petits fours and truffles as party favors for your guests to take home with them."

Talk about a one-eighty, Angela thought. "I'm honored you would volunteer to make the cake."

"It has nothing to do with honor. You're my grandbabies' mama."

"And you're my babies' Grammie. I'll let Viviana know you're interested in baking for the B and B. Do you mind if I give her your number so she can get in touch with you?"

"Of course I don't mind."

Rising to her feet, Angela walked over and dropped a kiss on Joyce's short gray curls. "Thank you."

Joyce stood. "I'll call you in a couple of days and whenever you're free I'd like to take you out to dinner."

"Where are we going?"

"Anywhere you want. The invitation also extends to Leland."

Angela was slightly taken aback by Joyce's willingness to include Leland. "It's time I get to meet the boy who's going to be my grandbabies' new daddy. Better yet, why don't you bring him with you when you come to church. He's not a non-Christian, is he?"

She wanted to tell Joyce that Lee was a man, not a boy. "Of course not." She also wanted to remind Joyce that he'd attended a parochial school.

"I'll let you know about going out to eat because I signed up to volunteer at the nursing home in Mineral Springs until the twins are back. One of these Sundays y'all can come over after church for dinner. Leland's sister is welcome to come, too."

"I'll let them know." Angela kissed Joyce again. "My lunch hour is almost over and I have to get back to the clinic."

Angela pressed the intercom button on the telephone console and waited for the receptionist to answer. "Yes, Angela?"

"Maylis, please hold my calls."

"For how long?"

Angela shook her head. The woman was so literal

that she found herself having to oversimply everything for her. "For the rest of the afternoon."

"Okay."

"Thank you, Maylis." She had blocked out time to work on billing insurance companies for reimbursement.

She entered her password and pulled up a file on an insurance company. Her fingers moved quickly as she typed in the required information for each field. Angela lost track of time as she checked and rechecked what she'd entered. Several years ago the clinic had undergone a Medicaid audit that had lasted months. Her head popped up when she heard someone knocking on the closed door.

"Who is it?"

"It's Maylis, Angela. You asked me to hold your calls."

She slowly shook her head. "What is it?"

"There's someone here asking to see you. He's in the waiting room."

"Tell him I'm coming." Angela saved the work and left her office. They had another two hours before the receptionist locked the door behind the last patient. With wide eyes, she stared at Lee. He wore a business suit.

He approached her and cupped her elbow. "Is there someplace we can go and talk?"

She nodded. "Yes. Come to my office." Angela unlocked the door to the hallway leading to exam rooms, her office and the private offices of Drs. Franklin and Hawkins. She smiled at the X-ray technician. Stepping aside, she allowed Lee to enter the space with barely enough room for a desk, love seat and side table.

Lee reached for her left hand. "I have to leave for Seattle."

Angela's body stiffened in shock. "Why?"

"One of my buddies who graduated Ranger School with me was involved in a head-on accident. His pickup caught fire and he would've died if several good Samaritans hadn't risked their lives to extricate him before the car exploded. He was airlifted to a burn center with severe head trauma and burns over the lower half of his body. His wife says he's now in a medically induced coma."

Angela remembered an adolescent boy running into the clinic, screaming in pain after he'd sustained burns to his face. Dr. Franklin had quickly assessed he had second-degree burns and directed the EMTs to transport him to the county hospital's trauma unit. "At least he's not aware of the pain."

Lee nodded. "I don't know how long I'm going to be away, and now with Vivi going on vacation I don't feel comfortable about you staying at the house by yourself."

"I think you're overreacting. If you were staying at The Falls House you would know Viviana had the place wired once she closed the boardinghouse. All I have to do is sync the security system with my phone, and if I see or detect anything suspicious I'll dial 911." There were no-delay sensors on the rear and side doors and motion detectors positioned in easily accessible areas.

"You're right. I am overreacting." Releasing her hand, he reached into the pocket of his jacket, and removed a small, velvet box. "I hadn't planned to give this to you until Friday." Lee opened the top to reveal a magnificent emerald-cut ruby ring surrounded by brilliant blue-white diamonds.

Angela clapped a hand over her mouth. "Oh, no!" she repeated over and over. Grasping her left hand, he slipped the ring on her finger. It was a perfect fit. "It's beautiful. When did you buy it? Why now? How did you get my ring size?" The words were tumbling over one another.

Cradling her face between his palms, Lee gently kissed her mouth, and then went down on one knee. "Will you do me the honor of becoming my wife?"

Tears flooded her eyes as she struggled not to cry. "Yes, I will."

Lee rose and kissed her again. "I have to go."

Angela fisted her hands to stop their trembling. "How are you getting to the airport?"

"A driver is outside waiting for me. I'll call you once we're on the ground."

"Be safe."

Lee angled his head and flashed a smile that did not quite reach his luminous eyes, and Angela knew he was worried about his buddy. He had buried one friend and she prayed he wouldn't have to stand at the graveside of another soldier.

He took her hands and kissed her fingers. "I will."

Turning on his heel, he walked out of the office, leaving Angela staring at his broad shoulders until he disappeared from her line of vision. She closed the door and sat down again. Instead of resuming billing, she swiveled on the chair and stared out the window overlooking the rear parking lot. The joy of wearing her fiancé's engagement ring paled when she thought of what his friend's wife was going through. She had been there herself.

Once Justin made the decision to drop out of medical school and enlist he'd talked at length about the pros and cons of becoming a soldier. He wasn't certain whether he would be deployed and took out additional insurance in case something happened to him. Angela remembered becoming inconsolable when she accused him of being fatalistic, but he must have had a premonition about dying.

And when word reached her that her husband had given his life in the service of his country she had gone completely numb. She'd wanted to cry but couldn't. It wasn't until she saw his flag-draped casket that she was able to accept that she was a widow, carrying two babies who would never see their father.

The sunlight coming through the window fired the blood-red stone and diamonds on her hand. It was the second time she'd accepted a marriage proposal. The first was from a man who chose the military over medicine, and the second had given up his military career to support his sister. Voices in the parking lot shattered her reverie and she once again focused on billing.

Angela woke when she heard the programmed ringtone. She'd attempted to stay up and wait for Lee's call. He'd left her a text that he had arrived safely and would contact her later.

She glanced at the time on the phone. It was minutes after midnight, which meant it was nine o'clock in Seattle. "Hello."

"Did I wake you, babe?"

"I was just dozing," she lied.

"No, you weren't. You were asleep."

She exhaled an audible sigh. "Yeah."

"I'm sorry, Angela. Go back to sleep. I'll call you tomorrow."

"It's already tomorrow." Now she was wide awake. "How's your buddy?"

"He's still in a coma. Doctors say he's critical, but they expect him to pull through. Even with the burns and two broken legs, his vitals are stable. It's his wife who's a mess. She had to be sedated."

"Where are you staying?"

"I'm spending the night at her house along with three other guys. Richie's parents and his sister and brother-in-law are flying in from Ohio and will be here tomorrow afternoon. Once they get here I'm going to check in to a hotel."

"Tell Richie's wife I'm going to say a prayer for her husband's recovery."

"I'm certain she'll appreciate all the prayers that come her way."

"Lee?"

"Yes?"

"I miss you."

"I miss you, too."

"Good night."

"Sleep tight."

A beeping sound indicated Lee had ended the call. Angela shifted onto her side and closed her eyes.

Sleep had become her enemy. She tossed and turned and when she finally woke the twisted sheets bore the evidence of her restlessness. She lay in bed until the alarm on her phone went off. It was time for her to get up and get ready for work.

* * *

Lee knew he'd shocked Angela when she saw him leaning against her Honda's bumper. He'd reserved a car to take him from the Charleston airport to Wickham Falls. Separated by three thousand miles and a three-hour time difference, he'd been forced to examine the depth of his feelings for the woman who'd accepted his proposal.

Many years ago, he'd sat in the school cafeteria pretending interest in his notes or a textbook when he'd surreptitiously stared at a tall, beautiful girl with a quick smile and a hypnotically modulated voice sitting at the next table with a boy he'd assumed was her boyfriend. Then, one day he'd glanced up to find her looking directly at him. There was something in her eyes that enthralled him and it was the first time he experienced a teenage crush.

Lee knew firsthand how some residents in The Falls resented anyone with Wolfe blood. And his father's criminal behavior had further tainted the family. He knew people were waiting for him to mess up while he was determined to prove them wrong. He stood straight, extended his arms and wasn't disappointed when Angela came into his embrace.

Angela couldn't believe her eyes when she saw Lee with a black leather carry-on. She'd spoken to him earlier that morning and he hadn't mentioned he was coming home. Going on tiptoe, she kissed his stubble. "Why didn't you tell me you were coming back?"

He stared at her under lowered lids. "What happened to *welcome home*?"

"Welcome home."

"That's better. I wanted to surprise you."

"You succeeded." She traced the outline of his eyebrow with her forefinger. "You look exhausted."

"I admit to being a little sleep-deprived."

Angela pressed the button on the handle of the van, unlocking the doors. "Get in. I'm taking you home."

Lee picked up his carry-on. "Will you spend the night with me?"

She heard a pleading in his voice and knew he didn't need to be alone. Whenever she asked about his friend, he claimed nothing had changed. That it would be a while before the doctors would bring him out of the coma and monitor his discomfort with pain medication. Angela wondered if Lee was thinking about his father, whose downward spiral into drug addiction had begun with the opioids prescribed to him in the VA hospital.

"I'll spend as many nights with you as you want," she said quietly.

Cupping the back of her head with his free hand, Lee lowered his head and kissed her until she struggled to breathe. "Let's go home."

Lee was exhausted but he didn't want to sleep until he made love to the woman lying next to him. He managed to shower and brush his teeth without falling on his face and got into bed while Angela unpacked his bag and put up a load of laundry. He dozed off and on while she showered and then got into bed with him. He hadn't bothered to close the drapes and light from a near-full moon silvered the space in an eerie glow.

It wasn't the first time they would share a bed, but tonight it was different for him. He had forced himself not to make love to Angela until she wore his ring. The ruby and diamond symbolized love and commitment and his desire to grow old with her.

Turning to face her, he rested a hand on her belly under one of his T-shirts.

Lee reversed their positions and pressed her body down on the mattress. Lowering his head, he nuzzled her neck. "I didn't make love to you because I didn't want you to think I only wanted you for sex."

"I was under the assumption you wanted to wait until we're married."

He trailed kisses along the column of her silken scent neck. "You assumed wrong, princess. There's no way I could remain celibate around you and not lose my mind." His hand slipped between her legs and covered her mound.

"I'm not on birth control."

Lee shifted slightly and reached over to open the drawer in the bedside table and took out a condom. "Don't worry, babe. I'll take care of it."

Angela experienced the full range of foreplay for the first time since becoming sexually active. Lee had kept his promise to sample her body as if she were a smorgasbord, starting with nibbling that began with her mouth and then every inch of her body until he tasted the soles of her feet. She quivered at the tenderness of his kiss and when he slipped on the condom, parted her legs and entered her, she surrendered completely to the erotic pleasure she had forgotten existed. Passion swept through her like a lit fuse, burning hotter and brighter until she felt something explode inside her in a brilliant shower of ecstasy. She still hadn't returned from her sensual free fall when Lee groaned out his own plea-sure as they climaxed simultaneously.

They lay together, still joined, enjoying the after-math of a shared fulfillment making them one with the other. "I love you." The three words she'd wanted to tell him days before slipped out unbidden.

Lee raised his head and stared at her. "Do you know long I've waited for you to tell me that you love me?"

Angela shook her head. "No. How long has it been, Lee?"

"Fifteen years. I fell in love with you before you came over and introduced yourself."

Angela cradled Lee's face. "A few times I'd ask my-self how different my life would've been if I'd met you first."

"How much different would it be?"

"I wouldn't be a widow."

"You forget that I am also a soldier."

"You *were* a soldier, and now you're a civilian. And please don't repeat what guys in the Corps claim—*once a marine, always a marine*—and say it's the same with an army ranger."

He kissed her nose. "The only thing I'm going to say is that good things come to those who wait." He pulled out. "I'm going to the bathroom to throw away the con-dom."

Angela rose slightly and stared at his magnificent nude body. The older Lee had opened up and revealed things about himself she never would've or could've imagined. He'd admitted to being mature enough to be-come a husband and father, and he'd just demonstrated that by talking to her instead of shutting her out. If she had one pet peeve about her first husband, then it was his inability to openly communicate with her.

She closed her eyes and waited for Lee to come back to bed. She smiled when his warmth enveloped her as he rested an arm over her hip. "Good night, darling."

"Sleep tight, princess."

Chapter Eleven

Angela hugged her children so tightly they squirmed to get away from her. Six weeks had passed quickly and she had driven to Charleston to meet her parents' flight from Los Angeles. She was disappointed when her father revealed they had booked at flight from Charleston to Daytona Beach for later that afternoon instead of spending a couple of days in Wickham Falls.

Holding on to her son and daughter's hands, she met her mother's eyes. "What on earth have you been feeding them? They've grown at least an inch since I last saw them."

Emmaline Banks smiled. Still very attractive at sixty, the college English professor ruffled Malcolm's hair. "Their Aunt Cassidy, who's now a total vegetarian, introduced them to dishes they would've normally turned their noses up at."

Angela's brother, Nathan Jr., or Nat, for short, had

married a California girl who was a yoga teacher and health fanatic.

She stared at her father. Nathan Banks, Sr., who'd been appointed dean of student affairs by college trustees, had shaved his head when he began balding several years ago. He'd recently added a neatly barbered mustache and goatee to his sculpted, angular face. Angela always felt her genes had compromised when she inherited her father's height and complexion, and her mother's features and hair texture, while her twins hadn't inherited any of the Bankses' physical characteristics.

Emmaline reached for Angela's left hand. "It's beautiful, sweetheart. I hope he makes you happy."

She blushed. "He does. I'd wanted you to stay a few days so you could get to know Lee better."

"Don't worry, baby girl," Nathan said, smiling. "Make sure you let us know once you set the date. We'll try and take off a couple of days before to help with whatever you need to make your big day special."

"Thanks, Daddy."

"Your mother and I will wait with the kids while you go and get your car. Then we're going through security to get something to eat before we have to board our next flight."

She hunkered down to the twins' height. "I'm going to get the van, then I'll be back to take you to see Grammie."

Zoe looked around her. "Where's Grammie?"

"She's home waiting for you."

Angela walked out of the terminal to the lot where she'd parked the minivan. Her parents had checked the car seats and the kids' luggage to Charleston. She retrieved her vehicle and when she stopped curbside her parents were waiting outside. Her father helped her secure the car seats, and within minutes Malcolm and Zoe were seated and strapped in. She stored their bags with colorful animated characters in the cargo area, hugged and kissed her mother, and then her father. They waited, waving to her as she pulled away from the curb and into traffic leading to the airport exit.

She was going to live with her mother-in-law again until repairs to The Falls House were completed. Angela had stayed with Lee until it came time for her children to return home. She'd told Joyce that she was moving back with the twins until she and Lee married, then they were moving permanently to the bed-and-breakfast.

Joyce appeared overjoyed to once more have her grandbabies under her roof. She had met with Viviana and agreed to provide the baked goods for the bed-and-breakfast.

It had been two weeks since work had begun on the newly incorporated Wickham Falls Bed-and-Breakfast. Lee drove over to meet the construction crew who arrived at six in the morning to begin repairing and renovating the interiors while another team arrived two hours later to concentrate on the exterior. Viviana, having returned from her cruise, had temporarily moved into one of the guesthouses.

"Mama, I'm sleepy," Zoe said, as she tried to stifle a yawn.

Angela glanced up at the rearview mirror. "Go to sleep, baby. It's going to be a while before we get home. You should also take a nap, Malcolm. I'll wake you when we get to Grammie's house." The drive from the state capital to The Falls took an hour, barring traffic delays.

"Okay, Mama."

She knew the twins missed their overindulgent paternal grandmother. There wasn't anything they asked for that Joyce didn't try to give them.

Joyce was waiting on the porch when she pulled into the driveway. She came down. "I can't believe they've grown so much in just a few weeks."

Angela unsnapped their harnesses. "That's what I told my mother." She woke Zoe and took her out of the seat. "You're going to have to stand up like a big girl," she said when the child's knees buckled slightly. Her parents had gotten them up early to make it to the airport.

Malcolm woke with wide eyes and spotted his grandmother. "Grammie!"

Zoe came alert. "Grammie!"

Joyce took Zoe's hand. "Come give Grammie a kiss."

The little girl made a big show of planting a noisy kiss on her grandmother's cheek. "Umm-ma!"

Angela helped Malcolm out of his seat and he rushed over to hug Joyce's knees. "I missed you, Grammie."

Joyce patted his curly hair. "And I missed you, too. Come in the house and wash up."

Zoe rubbed her eyes. "I'm sleepy, Grammie." Joyce took each child by the hand and led them up the steps and into the house.

Angela retrieved the luggage from the cargo area and followed them inside. She would miss sleeping with Lee but having her children back filled her with an indescribable joy.

Lee sat on a rocker on the wraparound porch, staring at the tiny birds chattering and splashing in the marble urn filled with water from the prior night's fast-moving thunderstorm. It had become his favorite spot to relax over the past week. The engineer had completed his report, confirming the house and the guesthouses were structurally sound, and within days the foreman of a home improvement firm arrived with his workers and reassured Lee that if his men put in ten-hour days and with a skeleton crew working Saturdays he would be able to complete the renovation mid-September.

Lee's impatience, unlike his sister's, did not focus on opening the B and B, but marrying Angela and living under one roof with her and her children. He had become accustomed to her sharing his bed at the extended stay, but that had changed when he moved into The Falls House after she returned to live with her children and mother-in-law.

A soft click punctuated the quietness of the early morning and he looked over his shoulder to find Viviana balancing a cup and saucer in each hand. "Don't get up," she urged when he rose from the rocker. She handed him a cup of coffee and then folded her body down on a chair facing his.

"Thanks. What are you doing up so early this morning?" It was only 6:30. Viviana usually didn't get up until after eight to prepare breakfast for them.

"When you told me Giles Wainwright and his cousin are coming over at eleven I thought I'd put together a little snack. There's nothing worse than discussing business while your stomach is making noises because you need sustenance."

"What do you consider a snack?" And knowing Viviana her snack could be anything from a three-course meal to caviar on toast points. He stared at his sister as he took a sip of the vanilla-flavored brew. He much preferred Mexican or Jamaican coffees to the flavored varieties.

A mysterious smile softened her mouth. "I can't decide whether to make a fruit and cheese platter, crudités, or skewered meats and shrimp with accompanying sauces."

"The Wainwrights are coming here to talk about purchasing land, not to chow down, Vivi."

Viviana set her coffee on the glass-topped all-weather table next to her chair. "Folks are usually more receptive and relaxed in discussing business if there's food and drink. The house may look a mess because of the work that's being done, but that shouldn't preclude us from showing the Big Apple Wainwrights some Southern cordiality."

His sister's words reminded Lee that she was the one trained in hotel management and hospitality. That she had been the go-to person to set up meetings and had doubled as the backup banquet manager when employed at a local hotel. He knew Viviana didn't need his input when it came to operating the bed-and-breakfast. What she needed was money to make the new business a reality and make it sustainable.

The month before the certificate of deposit had matured and instead of rolling it over Lee had withdrawn the proceeds and deposited it into a business account under the newly formed corporation. And to avoid a repeat of Viviana's last financial crisis, Lee had authorized the bank to set up alerts on the account for any expenditure over one hundred dollars, and all checks were required to have two electronic signatures. He didn't want his sister to think he didn't trust her to run the business. It was that he was distrustful of others who just might take advantage of her openness and generosity.

"Fix whatever you want. And you're right. It wouldn't hurt to show our New York guests that we can be charming and hospitable."

Viviana picked up her cup. It rattled slightly when her hand shook. "I didn't want to bring it up because I don't need you growling at me, but I spoke to Dad yesterday. He said he'd finished whatever he was working on and was planning to come down again. I told him it's not a good time because of the work going on in the house."

"I'm not going to growl at you if you want to keep in touch with Emory. I have no right to interfere if you want a relationship with him."

Viviana stared at Lee as if he'd taken leave of his senses. "Are you all right?"

"Of course I'm all right. Why would you ask me that?"

Damp, black curls danced around her face as she shook her head. "I thought you hated him so much that you couldn't stand to be in the same room together."

"Don't get me wrong, Vivi. I don't hate anyone. I resent Emory for what he put our mother through. I resent that he was so selfish that all he ever thought about was Emory Remington. I do understand how he became addicted but what I don't understand is how he could desert his wife and children whom he claimed he loved."

Viviana's eyelids fluttered as she blinked back tears. "I asked him the same question and he said he loved Mama but drugs were his jealous mistress. Every time he tried to leave her she would lure him back, and claims that she finally let him go only after he went to prison. Dad said he went cold turkey and has been clean and sober for twenty years. He's been living in Philadelphia, painting and volunteering at a center focusing on high-risk youth."

Lee, stretching out his legs, crossed his feet at the ankles. "I'm glad he's finally gotten his life together." He was relieved his father was drug-free and that he was doing what he liked.

"Are you really serious, Lee, or are you saying that because you think that's what I want to hear?"

"Why are you making this all about you, Vivi? Emory decided a long time ago how he wanted to live his life. And only he can determine what he wants and needs for his future."

Viviana averted her head. "Does this mean you're going to forgive him?"

"Forgive him for what, Vivi? Forgive him for cheating on his wife with mistresses with names like heroin and crack cocaine, and for neglecting his kids because he was too cowardly to let them see him for what he was—a junkie? It's up to Emory to forgive himself for the pain he caused our mother when she needed him most. He wasn't a very good husband, but now that he's clean maybe he'll be given a second chance to be a good grandfather."

Viviana leaned forward. "Angela's pregnant." The query was a statement.

Lee felt his heart stop for a few seconds, and then start up again, beating wildly against his ribs. Although he'd used protection whenever he made love to Angela, there was always the possibility that he could've gotten her pregnant and she'd elected to tell his sister first.

"No," he replied, hoping he sounded more confident than he felt.

"So, why did you say that Dad could be a good grandfather?"

"When I marry Angela, her children will become my children and Emory a surrogate grandfather."

A hopeful expression lit up Viviana's eyes. "Does this mean you're going to invite him to your wedding?"

"I don't know yet."

Viviana squeezed her eyes tightly as tears overflowed and trickled down her face. "Dad said he will carry the pain he caused us to his grave. I know we can't turn back the clock but I'm trying not to judge him for what he's done."

Lee stood and pulled his sister to stand. He held her as she cried without making a sound. He knew she had a soft spot for their father and prayed Emory wouldn't hurt her again. She was seven when their mother passed away and it had hit Viviana hard because she claimed she had no mother and no father.

"You shouldn't have to judge him, Vivi. The next time he comes I promise to sit down with him and hopefully come to terms about the past." He kissed her forehead. "Go and buy whatever you need for your snack."

Viviana sniffled and swiped at her tears with the backs of her hands. "I'm sorry for losing it."

He angled his head, smiling. "There's no need to apologize."

Her expression brightened. "Would you mind if I invite Angela to join us? After all, she's going to become part of this family and she should know what's going on behind the scenes."

"Of course I don't mind."

Now that her children were back, Lee rarely got to see Angela. She had invited him to join them tomorrow for church services before going back to her mother-in-law's house for dinner. It was to be his first time interacting with the little boy and girl.

"I'm going to call her now."

Lee shook his head when Viviana reached into the pocket of her blouse and took out her cell phone. He picked up both coffee cups and managed to open the door without dropping them as the sound of his sister's laughter floated in the air. Nothing fired up Viviana more than entertaining. They'd been teasing each other that both had chosen the perfect career path. He had become the ultimate soldier and she the perfect hostess as an innkeeper.

Lee opened the door and nodded to Captain Giles Wainwright. He knew the man standing behind the former marine was his cousin, Noah. Noah was tall, with a mop of shaggy ash-blond hair falling over his ears and forehead. Giles had called to inform him Noah was in DC and had planned to take a side trip to The Falls before returning to New York.

"Please come in." Lee stood off to the side, watching the Wainwrights as they stared up at the entryway's soaring twenty-foot ceiling. He extended his hand to Giles and then his cousin. "Leland Remington."

The blond, who looked more like a California surfer than a real estate developer, took the proffered hand. "Noah Wainwright."

"Welcome to what will eventually become the Wickham Falls Bed-and-Breakfast. The work crew is currently on their lunchbreak, so we should be able to discuss business without have to shout to one another to be heard over the hammering and drilling. We'll talk in the solarium."

"How many rooms are in this house?" Noah asked as he followed Lee through the great room and down a hallway to the rear of the mansion, into a room resembling an indoor oasis.

"There are ten bedroom suites, five in each wing of the house." Lee waited for Giles and Noah to sit before taking his own seat. Bright sunlight came through the French doors of the solarium, turning it into an emerald forest. He pointed to the cloth-covered table with a number of small bowls of sauces. "The ladies of the house have put together a little repast to sustain us." As soon as the words were off his tongue Viviana and Angela walked into the solarium.

The three men came to their feet. Lee heard Noah's soft exhalation of breath as he stared at Viviana. He wanted to tell the man to close his mouth because he was practically salivating.

Moving quickly, Lee took a platter heaped with thinly sliced chicken, cubes of beef, snow-peas-wrapped shrimp, lamb and ginger-orange pork skewers from Angela and set it on the table next to the sauces. He winked at her when she met his eyes. She hadn't hesitated when Viviana called and asked her to help her put together a buffet for a luncheon business meeting.

He hadn't been able to take his eyes off her when she walked in wearing a pair of stretchy navy capris, a blue-and-white pinstriped tailored shirt, and navy leather low-heeled mules. She looked delightfully wholesome with a barely-there cover of makeup and her hair pulled back in a loose ponytail.

He put an arm around her waist. "Giles, you've already met Angela Mitchell and my sister, Viviana."

Giles nodded to Viviana. "It's good seeing you again. And congratulations, Angela, on your engagement."

Angela smiled. "You've heard about that?"

Attractive lines fanned out around Giles's brilliant blue eyes when he returned her smile. "The whole town's talking about it."

Lee tightened his hold on Angela's waist. "Giles, I'll leave it up to you to introduce your cousin."

Giles rested a hand on Noah's shoulder. The resemblance between the two men was noticeable. Both were tall with blue eyes. Giles's were clear, reminiscent of blue topaz, while Noah's were closer to aquamarine.

"I'd like you to meet my business counterpart and younger cousin, Noah Wainwright."

Noah took a step and offered Angela his hand. "It's my pleasure." He then turned to Viviana, who was holding a bottle of red and white wine in either hand. He took the bottles and set them down on the table. "I'm honored. It is Viviana, isn't it?"

She gave him a direct stare. "Yes, it is Viviana."

Lee noticed a vaguely sensuous light pass from the developer to his sister, and he wanted to tell Noah to turn off whatever signal he'd hoped to send her. Whenever he offered to set her up with one of his buddies, she would invariably inquire if he was blond because she was partial to dark-haired men.

Cupping Angela's elbow, Lee pulled out a chair at

the table and seated her, while Noah moved quickly to seat Viviana. He had to admit that his sister and fiancée had outdone themselves. They'd set the table with china, crystal, silver and serving pieces. They'd also prepared fruit and green salads along with the various skewered meats.

He pressed his shoulder to Angela's. "Do you want red or white wine?"

"White, please."

Wineglasses were filled and raised in a toast to new and old friends and success for the new B and B. Lee gave the Wainwrights the abridged version of the Wolfes' rise to power as owners of several very profitable coal mines in Johnson County. He was forthcoming when he revealed how the Wolfes had resisted workers' unions and hired a private army of goons to intimidate them. But it was a number of accidents, resulting in loss of life, and their refusal to install the safety measures mandated by the government that had finally brought down their empire.

"The Wolfes were still considered wealthy because they owned large parcels of land," Lee continued. "There was a time when this house and outbuildings sat on more than two hundred acres. Over the years they began selling off lots until we're left with twelve acres, eight of which I'd like to unload."

"Why?" Noah asked, speaking for the first time since sitting down opposite Viviana, as he continued to stare at her under lowered lids.

"Four acres is more than enough for our current lifestyle," Lee said.

"There was a time when our family did a lot of entertaining and every room in this house overflowed with family members and their guests," Viviana added. "People don't have large families like they did in the past, and that means Lee and I would have to have at least eight children between us to fill up all of the rooms if we hadn't turned half the house into a bed-and-breakfast. Then there are two guesthouses on the property with two-bedroom suites for any overflow."

Noah and Giles shared a glance. "Do you intend to keep the guesthouses?"

"Yes," Lee replied. "And if you're interested in purchasing the land, then I can give you the geologist's report from the last sale."

Crossing his arms over his chest, Noah leaned back in his chair. "If I decide to make you an offer, after I survey it, what do you propose I use it for?"

"I'd like to answer that question," Angela volunteered. All eyes were directed at her. "There's a shortage of modern affordable homes in Wickham Falls. I hadn't realized that until I began looking for a house for me and my children." She smiled at Noah. "You claim you're a developer."

Pale eyebrows lifted slightly. "So they say."

"As a developer you can either build eight middle-income or sixteen moderately-priced homes on one-or half-acre lots."

Giles tented his fingers. "I like the sound of that." He turned to Noah. "Maybe you should hire Angela as a consultant for the Wainwright Developers Group." He'd raised his voice to be heard because the hammering and drilling had started up again.

Angela shook her head. "Thank you, but no. I have a set of three-year-old twins, and I'm getting married in a few months. Leaving Wickham Falls on business isn't an option for me."

"I just thought I'd ask," Giles said.

Noah picked up a napkin and touched it to the corners of his mouth. "Perhaps I can look at what you're offering before we go even further." He stood up. "Viviana, would you mind showing me what I can expect to get for my money."

She blinked slowly and rose to her feet. "It rained last night, so the ground may still be a little damp. I'll be with you as soon as I change my shoes."

Noah nodded. "I'll wait for you on the porch."

Pushing back his chair, Giles also stood. "If you guys don't mind I'm going to have to walk off some of this food. I definitely ate too much. And if this is a sample of what you plan to serve your guests then you can look for me and Mya to check in every once in a while."

Angela waited until she and Lee were alone in the solarium to say, "I think Giles's cousin is smitten with your sister."

Lee traced the rim of his water goblet with his finger. "Poor dude. He has no idea that she's not interested."

"Why are you speaking for her, Lee? You told me about how her last boyfriend scammed her, and that's hardly going to happen with Noah Wainwright. I'm willing to bet the Wainwrights could buy every house in The Falls and still have money left over to pick up a few more in Mineral Springs."

Shifting on his chair, Lee turned to face Angela. "How do you know their net worth?"

"You're not the only one who uses Google," she

teased, reminding him of how he'd found the restaurant the night they went to the movies.

Lee ran a finger down the length of her nose. "You may not want to hear this, but don't get involved trying to play matchmaker with Vivi and Noah Wainwright. Unfortunately for him he'll soon find out the hard way that she's not impressed by his money or surfer-dude image."

"It sounds as if you don't want your sister to find somebody."

"That's where you're wrong, babe. I want more than anything for her to be as happy as we are."

"If that's the case, then don't interfere if something happens between her and Noah."

Lee gave her an incredulous look. "What's up with you and this dude?"

Angela's jaw dropped. "There's nothing going on with me and this dude, except I can see what you refuse to see. When I was modeling I saw a lot of wealthy men transfixed by some of the girls and I knew they weren't going to stop until they had them."

"What happened?"

"They wound up as their wives or their mistresses."

Lee pressed his fist to his mouth and Angela knew he was conflicted when it came to his sister because she'd dated several men who had used her. She'd just met Noah, but there was something about the man she liked. He projected an air of inner strength and quiet confidence.

"Having another Wainwright around will definitely benefit The Falls."

"What are you talking about?" Lee questioned.

"If Noah decides to buy the land and build homes,

then he will have to spend time here overseeing the project. The Wainwrights are known for their philanthropy. Thanks to the generosity of Giles and Sawyer Middleton we were able to open a drug treatment program with full-time and part-time substance abuse counselors. Seth's wife, Dr. Natalia Hawkins, volunteers her services as medical director, and now all first responders are required to carry naloxone to reverse the effects of a drug overdose."

"Hypothetically, if he does decide to build, there's no guarantee he'd want to live here permanently. Wickham Falls is culture shock to someone who grew up in New York City. And what makes you so certain he'd be willing to relocate?"

Leaning closer, Angela brushed her mouth over Lee's. "Call it woman's intuition."

Lee deepened the kiss. "Are you willing to bet on your so-called woman's intuition?"

She stared into the orbs that were more blue than gray. "Sure. What's the prize?"

"The winner gets to select where we go on our honeymoon."

Angela and Lee had talked about delaying taking a honeymoon until after the New Year. Joyce had volunteered to look after Malcolm and Zoe until they returned.

"Bet. Where do you want to go?" she asked Lee. "And remember we're only taking off a week"

"Bahia."

"Are you talking Bahia, Brazil?"

"Have you ever been to Brazil?" he asked.

Angela nodded as she recalled visiting the South American country. "I went there for a magazine swim-

suit layout and stayed for Carnival. I came home run-
down and dehydrated and took two months off before
working again."

"How old were you?"

"Just say I wasn't old enough to drink in the States.
You have to remember I began doing print ads at thir-
teen, and when I quit the business at twenty-five I'd
had more than a decade of parading in front of people."

"Would you discourage Zoe if she decides she wants
to model?"

"Of course I would. It's not as glamorous as it looks.
Most of the girls starve themselves and compromise
their health because they fear putting on a few pounds.
Anorexia and bulimia were the norm rather than the
exception."

Lee nibbled on her lower lip. "I'll back you up on
whatever you decide for our kids. Back to the wager.
Where do you want to go, princess?"

"I was thinking of Key West." It was one of Angela's favorite places to visit in the States. The other was
San Antonio, Texas.

"I love Key West."

"I guess that does it," she said with a smug grin.
"We'll honeymoon in Key West."

"Whoa, baby! What happened to the wager?"

"It's null and void because you said you love Key
West. Did you hear me say I love Bahia?"

"No, but—"

"No buts, darling," she interrupted softly. "I promise to make it so memorable that you'll want to go back
year after year."

Lee anchored his hands under her shoulders and
shifted her until she straddled his lap. Angela's arms

circled his neck and she pressed a kiss below his ear. Oh, how she missed him. The unleashed power in his arms when he lifted her easily, the firmness of his masterful mouth able to bring her to heights of passion she'd never experienced, and the hypnotic smell of his cologne that complemented his natural masculine scent. And she didn't want to think how much she'd missed his lovemaking, a lovemaking in which he made certain she climaxed before he did, or the rare times when it occurred simultaneously.

He laughed and nuzzled her ear. "Will I have to use a safe word?"

Angela moved sensuously, simulating a lap dance as she combed her fingers through his thick, black wavy hair. It was her turn to laugh when a groan slipped from his parted lips. "It all depends." Throwing back his head, Lee continued to groan as he closed his eyes. She kissed his throat. "Let me get up before someone walks in on us."

"You hump me, get me aroused, and now you want me to let you go."

"Please, Lee."

He released her and she slipped off his lap and began the task of clearing the table. Lee followed and stood behind her. "Don't move."

Angela closed her eyes when she felt the bulge against her hips. She and Lee hadn't made love in more than two weeks. Her children were back, and repairs to the proposed bed-and-breakfast had begun in earnest to restore the exterior to it former splendor. Improvement to the interior included updating plumbing and electrical, scraping and refinishing parquet flooring, and removing and replacing wall coverings.

"That was close," Lee breathed in her ear. "The next time you decide to give me a lap dance I'd appreciate it if you'd do it where we can have complete privacy."

She smiled at him over her shoulder. "Okay." Angela had just removed the tablecloth when Viviana and Noah returned. Her future sister-in-law's face was flushed with high color as she laughed at something he'd said to her.

Holding the cloth to her chest, Angela smiled at them. "How was the walk?"

"Good," Viviana said.

"Good and quite interesting," Noah added. He glanced around the solarium. "Where's Giles?"

Lee entered the room. "He said he was going for a walk. Why don't you wait on the porch?" he suggested. "He couldn't have gone that far."

"I'd like to talk to my cousin before setting up another meeting with you. I know tomorrow's Sunday, and I have reservations to fly back to New York early Monday morning, but can you set aside some time so we can talk before I leave?"

Lee met Angela's eyes. "I've committed to attend church services with my family, and then have dinner with Angela's mother-in-law. Maybe we can get together afterward."

"Do you go to church, Noah?" Angela asked him.

He flashed a sheepish smile. "Not as often as I used to, much to my mother's disappointment."

Giles walked into the solarium in time to overhear Noah. "I told my cousin that once he becomes a family man he'll give up partying and set a good example for his kids by taking them to church. Mya and I usually attend the early service so we can have the rest of the day to relax."

"I asked you, Noah," Angela continued, "because maybe you can come to church with us, and then you and Lee can talk business while my mother-in-law and I prepare dinner."

Giles gave Noah a pointed look. "Try and wiggle out of that invitation, little cuz."

Angela saw Lee give her a barely perceptible nod of approval. Angela knew how important it was for him to sell off the land to cover cost overruns, future unforeseen emergencies and have enough cash on hand for the off-season.

"Giles, why don't you come with Mya and Lily so it can be a family affair?"

"Are you certain your mother-in-law won't mind?" Giles asked.

"Her passion is cooking for other people. I'll call her later to set out a few more plates."

"It's been a long time since I've gone to church," Noah mumbled. "I just hope the roof stays on."

Angela laughed along with the others. "Don't worry about the roof, Noah. It's less than a year old."

"We'll see you in church tomorrow," Viviana crooned in a singsong. She looped her arm through Angela's and pulled her in the direction of the kitchen. "You were amazing!"

Her brow furrowed. "What are you talking about?"

"You got Noah to agree to attend services. Did you see his face when you invited him to come to church with us? I thought he was going to pass out."

"He could've refused."

Viviana shook her head. "I doubt that. Once you mentioned he could build homes I could see the wheels turning in his head. And when he saw the undeveloped acreage he closed his eyes and didn't move for about two minutes. I thought he'd gone into a trance. But then he opened his eyes and said, *'I want it, and how much are you asking?'* I told him he'd have to talk to my brother. When Lee and I set up the new corporation we agreed I would be president and secretary and he vice-president and treasurer. I'm going to have my hands full running the B and B and supervising staff. And Lee was always better at handling money than I."

Angela was glad Viviana knew her financial limitations where it concerned running a business. She, on the other hand, used the same investment management company as her parents, and was always consulted before recommending an investment. She smiled at her future sister-in-law. "It sounds like a win-win for the both of you."

"No, Angela. It's a win-win-win for the three of us, because all of our wishes are about to come true. Lee's going to marry the woman he's always loved. And I may sound biased because he's my brother, but you're going to get a husband who will put your happiness and those of your children first, and I'll get a second chance to become a successful innkeeper."

An expression of satisfaction shimmered in Angela's eyes. Leland Remington's return to Wickham Falls had been totally unexpected, and she had reconnected with him as if the four years since their last encounter was four seconds. The uncomplicated camaraderie she'd shared with Lee in high school was still evident. And the friends-for-life pledge she, Justin and Lee had made would result in her marrying her late husband's best friend.

"Speaking of marriages, I'm going to need your help pulling off a miracle."

"Don't sweat it, Angela. You have the venue, so that's one thing you can cross off your list. I still have contacts with several local caterers, floral designers and DJs from my days as assistant banquet manager at the hotel in town that was bought out by a larger chain. Once you and Lee set a date and send out invitations I'll contact my sources."

"Miss Joyce offered to make the wedding cake."

"There you go," Viviana drawled. "You're all set."

Angela went through a mental list of what she needed for her special day. "I still have to select a gown. I want it very simple," she said quickly. "No beading or ruffles."

"Do you have a theme?"

She wanted to tell Viviana that she hadn't had to concern herself with a theme or any of the accoutrements that went along with planning a wedding when she and Justin had a courthouse ceremony. Angela knew she'd disappointed her parents, particularly her father, who wasn't given the privilege of walking his daughter down the aisle and giving her away.

"We'll probably marry early October, and I think a fall harvest theme would be in keeping with the season."

Viviana nodded, reminding Angela of a bobblehead doll. "Give me a few days to create something spectacular."

Angela didn't want spectacular, she wanted simple, but didn't have the heart to stifle Viviana's enthusiasm.

She had been through enough with her lowlife ex, and it was time for her to smile and start over again, this time with the support of her loved ones.

Chapter Twelve

"I think it's time you sat down and put your feet up," Angela said to Joyce. "When Viviana and Mya get through putting the kids down for a nap they'll help me clean up the kitchen."

Joyce tried unsuccessfully to stifle a yawn. "I'm good."

"No, you're not good. I know you're exhausted because you were dozing off during the pastor's sermon."

"I was just resting my eyes."

"You were resting your eyes for more than five minutes? You went to bed late and woke up early this morning. And you outdid yourself today. Everything was delicious."

When Angela called Joyce to tell her she'd invited four more guests to dinner the normally unflappable woman had panicked. She claimed the roasting chicken wasn't big enough to feed seven adults and three children. Angela had offered to make molasses-braised beef short ribs from her mother's recipe, which assuaged Joyce's anxiety.

Joyce flashed a weak smile. "I guess I am a little tired. Before I go I just want to say that Leland grew up to be a fine young man. I guess he got that from his mama."

Angela groaned inwardly. "Please don't go there. You promised me you weren't going to judge him."

"I'm not judging him. I like him and your friends." Joyce took off her bibbed apron and placed it over the back of a chair. "After I get up we'll have coffee and cake."

Viviana walked into the kitchen. "Mya's still trying to get Lily to fall asleep."

Angela smiled. "My kids are like Rip Van Winkle. They fall asleep quickly and stay asleep until you wake them up."

"Your kids are adorable. I passed the family room and the guys look as if they're having a serious conversation."

Angela filled the sink with hot soapy water as Viviana stacked plates and set them in the water. "Buying and selling land takes a lot of negotiating."

"I know. That's why Lee is involved and not me."

"What did I miss?" Mya asked, as she joined Angela and Viviana.

Angela smiled at Giles's wife. She'd given up her career as a college English instructor to become a stay-at-home mother. Loose brown curls with reddish highlights framed a tawny face with large hazel eyes.

"Noah's negotiating with my brother to buy some land we don't use."

Mya picked up several glasses. "If it's real estate, then you're singing the Wainwrights' song. They eat, sleep, walk and talk land deals. Noah is sort of the odd man out in the family because not only is he a developer, but he's also an architect."

"Giles isn't an architect?" Viviana questioned.

"No. He's an engineer. The Wainwright Developers Group happens to be the second largest real estate company in the northeast and their goal is to make it number one."

Viviana whistled under her breath. "How is it being married to a Wainwright?"

"It can be overwhelming and intoxicating at the same time. Are you thinking about joining the family, Viviana? I did notice Noah staring at you."

A flush suffused Viviana's face. "No. I just got out of a very toxic relationship and right now I'm done with men."

"Even if you were looking, I wouldn't set you up with Noah because he's quite the party animal who has a reputation of breaking up with his girlfriends the moment they mention the *M*-word."

Viviana waved her hand. "I wouldn't date him anyway because he's not my type. I'm not attracted to blond men."

Angela shared a questioning look with Mya. She had never had a type when it came to a man. She had only dated two men and both were very different in appearance and personality.

Lee had established the habit of going to Miss Joyce's house to read to Malcolm and Zoe before they went to bed. Angela had given him a collection of children's books and didn't take long for him to discover their favorites.

He folded his body down to a beanbag chair in their bedroom and waited for them to emerge from the bathroom.

Zoe and Malcolm raced into the bedroom and joined Lee on the beanbag. He smiled. They smelled of soap and clean laundry. "Which one do you want me to read?"

"Morris the Moose," they said in unison.

Lee rolled his eyes upward. He had lost count of the number of times they'd asked him to read about the moose. The book was one of their favorites because they had memorized most of the words. Zoe rested her head against his arm as he opened to the first page. "Today Morris—"

"It's not 'today,' Daddy," Zoe said. "It's 'one day.'"

"Yes. One day," Malcolm repeated, agreeing with his sister.

Lee still had to get used to the kids calling him Daddy. When Angela had introduced them she told her son and daughter that Lee was going to become their new daddy. Malcolm cheered but it was different with Zoe. She'd given him what Lee thought was a suspicious look. It was another two days before she finally called him Daddy because she wanted him to help her tie her tennis shoes.

He occasionally would change a word but found that he couldn't fool the three-year-olds. "Oops! I meant one day." He dropped a kiss on their heads. "You guys are so smart." Lee read slowly, mimicking the voices of the various animals and finishing the book when Angela walked into the bedroom. He winked at her as she sat on the window seat. "I'm going to read them one more story before you put them to bed." The children clapped their hands when he opened another one of their favorite books: "Dogs Don't Wear Sneakers."

"I like when you make animal sounds, Daddy," Malcolm said, smiling.

Lee ruffled the boy's curly hair. "One of these days I'm going to take you to a petting zoo so you can see the animals we read about."

"Will we see a moose?" Zoe asked.

"No, baby girl. Moose are in big zoos with lions, tigers and elephants."

Malcolm scrambled off the beanbag. "Mama, can we go to a zoo?"

Angela stood. "We'll start with the petting zoo before we visit one with wild animals."

Lee pushed to his feet, bringing Zoe up with him. "Storytime is over and it's time for you munchkins to go to bed."

Angela mouthed a thank-you as the twins walked over to their beds, knelt down and recited their prayers. He walked out of the house and sat on the porch to wait for Angela. He had surprised himself that he'd taken to parenting like a duck to water, and bonding with Malcolm and Zoe went a lot smoother than he had anticipated. The children were bright, even-tempered and curious, and he still couldn't believe his good fortune once he realized he was going to marry the woman he'd always loved and become a father to their children.

Lee stood in the doorway, watching his father close the distance between them. Emory had called Viviana to say he was in between jobs and wanted to see her again. There were only minor repairs left before they were able to open the bed-and-breakfast to the public, Lee had told her to invite him to stay. When he heard the phrase "in between jobs," he wondered if his father had relapsed and had picked up odd jobs to sustain himself.

So much had changed for Lee in the three months since he'd come back to Wickham Falls: he'd opened up to Angela about loving her; she'd accepted his marriage proposal, and they planned to exchange vows in two weeks; he'd moved back to the house where he'd grown up, and sold off the eight acres to the Wainwright Developers Group for much more than he would've gotten at auction.

He did not realize he'd been holding his breath, and let it out slowly when he came face-to-face with the man he rarely thought of as Dad. Lee had to admit Emory looked better now than when he saw him in mid-June. His face was fuller, but there was a look in his eyes that Lee believed was uneasiness.

Lee smiled. "You look good."

Emory stared at his son. "So do you."

"Come in. Can I get you something to eat?"

"No, thank you. I ate before leaving Philly." Emory looked around the entryway. "The house looks wonderful. You've brought it back to life."

Lee looked over his shoulder to find his father staring at the textured wallcoverings that had replaced the floral prints. "Vivi consulted an interior decorator to update the house without losing its original character. We'll talk in the drawing room." He led him into the room where guests could gather in the evening before retiring for bed.

"I saw the Opening Soon sign advertising the house as the Wickham Falls Bed-and-Breakfast. When's the big day?"

Lee waited for Emory to sit in an armchair, and then sat on a matching love seat facing him. "It won't be until after my wedding."

The older man went completely still. "You're getting married?" Lee nodded. "When I spoke to Viviana she didn't say anything to me."

"In two weeks I'll marry a local girl I went to high school with. She's a military widow with three-year-old twins."

Resting his head against the back of the chair, Emory closed his eyes. "I know your marriage will be nothing like what I had with your mother." When he opened them they were shimmering with unshed tears.

Lee listened without interrupting as Emory talked about the demons brought on by his addictions. When he couldn't get his drugs, he drank until he passed out. He talked about falling in love with Annette Wolfe at first sight when he saw her walk across the college quadrangle. They had dated for three months and once Annette told him she was pregnant they decided to marry.

"That's when we both dropped out of college and she said we had to live with her folks." He paused. "I'll never forget the look on her father's face when I introduced myself as her husband. They wouldn't allow me to stay in this house, so I told Annette either she could come with me or stay. She opted to come. I've asked myself ten thousand times would things have been different if she had stayed."

"That still wouldn't change the fact that she had an

inoperable brain tumor," Lee said, speaking for the first time.

"That's true, but what was left of her life would've been so different."

"Of course it would. She wouldn't have had me and Vivi."

A hint of a smile touched the corners of Emory's mouth. "You're right about that."

"What about now, Dad? How has your life changed?"

"I served my time, and once I was paroled I was too embarrassed to come back here. I got permission from my parole officer to move to Philadelphia where I found work as a housepainter. I met a woman who agreed to be my sponsor. She encouraged me to enroll in adult education art courses at a local junior college. She helped me sell my first painting to a prestigious Philly art gallery. Several more are in private collections and more than a dozen hang in various modern art museums around the country. Although I've received modest success as an abstract artist I would give it all up if I could get my family back."

Emory did not know if he had forgiven him. What Lee wasn't able to do was forget the pain, the loneliness and the fear of abandonment by a man who should have been there to protect him and his sister after their mother died. He knew none of them could erase the past and that meant he, Emory and Viviana had to move forward toward reconciliation.

"Getting your family back is going to be a work in progress. Meanwhile you can stay in one of the guesthouses for as long as you want." Emory pressed his fist to his mouth, a gesture Lee realized he also affected. "Wait here and I'll get the keys. I'm putting you in the first guesthouse along the path because there's still work to be done in the other one."

"When am I going to meet this very special woman who has captured my son's heart?" Emory asked when Lee returned and handed him a set of keys.

"She called me just before you pulled up. She should be here at any moment."

Emory gave Lee a long, penetrating stare. "Do you love her?"

"Of course I love her. Why ask me that when I told you I'm marrying her?"

"I just wanted to make certain."

Lee's face clouded with uneasiness. Did his father actually believe he would marry a woman he didn't love? That he had an ulterior motive for asking Angela to become his wife? "What's behind this inquisition?"

Emory angled his head and crossed his arms over his chest. "Men marry for a lot of reasons—love being one of them, but then they also love other things that may threaten that marriage. For some it's other women, gambling or neglecting them because they prefer hanging out to coming home. It was drugs for me. You need to ask yourself what else do you love that may pull you away from your wife and children? Viviana told me you're an army ranger, and I know what you had to go through to earn that honor. Are you actually ready to embrace life as a civilian innkeeper?"

"I'm not the innkeeper. Vivi is."

"So, you're the groundskeeper?"

"No!" Lee struggled not to lose his temper. He and Emory hadn't been together more than fifteen minutes and they were already at odds with each other, because he felt Emory was in no position to offer fatherly advice. "I promised Vivi I would help her fix up this place so she could reopen again. When I put in for my discharge I'd planned to give myself a year before reenlisting."

"I had no idea you planned to reenlist."

Lee quickly came to his feet as if pulled up by a bungee cord. He hadn't heard Angela come in. "We'll talk about that later."

The smile that didn't reach her eyes was more of a sneer. "Yes, we will, darling."

He registered the condescension in her voice. Although they didn't agree on everything, he and Angela were usually able to come to a compromise. And Lee hadn't broached the possibility of reenlisting with her because he wanted to take all the time given him to cement the bond between him and his wife and children.

Lee walked over to Angela and rested a hand at the small of her back. "Dad, I'd like you to meet Angela."

Emory ignored Angela's proffered hand and kissed her cheek. "I'm honored to meet you, Angela."

She nodded. "Thank you. And I'm pleased that I can finally get to meet you, too."

Emory stared over Angela's head at Lee. "I'm going to the car to get my bags, and then turn in for the night. Angela, will I see you tomorrow?"

"Of course you will. I'm extending an invitation for you to join us for dinner tomorrow so you can get to meet my mother-in-law and children."

"I'm looking forward to meeting your family."

Angela waited for Emory to leave before rounding on Lee. "I don't believe you!"

He blinked once. "What don't you believe?"

"We've been engaged since July and now it's October, and not once did you hint that you were going to reenlist. What do they say? That the wife or girlfriend is always the last to know?"

"I was going to tell you."

"When were you going to tell me? After I become Mrs. Leland Wolfe Remington and you finally get what you always wanted?"

"You knew I was a soldier when you agreed to marry me."

"Must I keep reminding you that you *were* a soldier, Leland? When I asked you how long you were going to stay in Wickham Falls I remember you saying it was 'indefinite,' which implied you weren't going to reenlist in the Army. I married one soldier and I swore I'd never marry another one. I have no intent of becoming a two-time military widow. Some women collect engagement and wedding rings. I don't want to be the one to collect triangular-folded flags." Her chest rose and fell as she struggled to draw a normal breath. "You have exactly one week to figure out what you want or the wedding is off. One week, Leland. And in case you can't count, that's seven days."

All traces of blue disappeared in Lee's eyes. "You're being unreasonable."

"Am I, Leland? If you'd intended to become a lifer, then you should've told me, otherwise I never would have agreed to marry you." Angela knew she had hit a nerve when he recoiled as if she had struck him across the face. "There is life after the military. All you have to do is look at Sawyer who now teaches technology. Then there's Aiden who came back to work at his family's restaurant. And don't forget your new buddy Giles, who is involved in real estate. You're a bright guy who graduated at the top of our class, so why don't you do something with your military benefits and go to college and get a career that doesn't include covert missions." She turned on her heel and walked out, leaving Lee staring at her back.

Angela waited until she was a block from her house when the tears she had held in check fell. She didn't blame Lee as much as she blamed herself for agreeing to marry less than five months after reuniting. They had planned to exchange vows the second Saturday in October. Sitting in the car and staring out the windshield she wondered if she'd agreed to marry for all the wrong reasons: loneliness and gaining a father for her children.

She exhaled a ragged sigh. Zoe and Malcolm adored Lee. They were all over him the instant he walked through the door. He took turns riding them on his shoulders as he pretended he was a horse, all the while making neighing and snorting sounds, and reading to them at night before they went to bed.

Angela glanced at the ruby-and-diamond ring on her left hand. She prayed she wasn't being unreasonable for issuing a deadline. She loved him, loved him more than she believed she could love a man. It had taken her a while to admit that she'd loved Justin, but it was a different love with Leland.

For the most part her relationship with Lee was drama-free. She'd found him to be even-tempered and controlled. But it was his passion she had come to look for. They didn't make love as often as she would've liked, and she was looking forward to the day when they would live under the same roof and sleep in the same bed.

Angela reached into her handbag and took out a tissue to blot the moisture on her face. She had to get herself together before walking into the house ablaze with lights, which told her Joyce had not retired for bed.

"Did you get to meet Leland's father?"

It was the first question Joyce asked as she walked through the door. "Yes. It's uncanny how much they resemble each other."

Joyce nodded. "When I saw him for the first time I understood why Annette married him. He was quite the head-turner."

"Like father, like son," Angela said under her breath. "I'm going to turn in early tonight. I have a final fitting for my gown tomorrow." A gown she wasn't certain she would ever wear.

"What's up, Lee?" Viviana asked her brother. "You've been moping around like someone who's lost their best friend. Or could it be your fiancée? And I noticed you haven't gone to Miss Joyce's for dinner in days. What's up with you, bro?"

"Stay out of this, Viviana. It doesn't concern you."

"Stay out of what!"

Lee glared at her. "My life."

"Life, Lee? Right now you don't seem to have one. You're up and out of the house before I get up and slink back when you believe I'm in bed. Even Dad mentioned that he rarely gets to see you and is planning to go back to Philadelphia before your wedding. I'll understand if you're experiencing PTSD. I'm here if you want my help."

"I don't have PTSD," he spat out.

Viviana ignored his acerbic retort. She sat on the

arm of Lee's chair and wrapped her arms around his neck. He hadn't shaved in days and the black stubble on his face matched his dark mood.

"Remember the day the doctor came to see Mama and he was in her bedroom for a long time before he told us we could go in?" Lee nodded. "She beckoned for us to sit on the side of her bed and it was a while before she was able to speak. Now that I look back I realize the doctor had given her something to make her very sleepy, and I still remember what she told us. She wanted us to always be there for each other, and never shut the other out because we only had each other. Even though Dad's back in our lives I still feel it's just you and me.

"And you were there for me when I called to tell you I was going to lose the house. You walked away from your military career and almost cleaned out your savings to help me. I can't repay you, Lee, and I don't know if I'll ever repay you."

"Did I ask you to repay me?"

Viviana rested her chin on the top of his head. "No, you didn't. I love you, Lee, and it pains me to see you like this. You can tell me it's none of my business again, but I have to ask. Are you still going to marry Angela?"

A beat passed. "I don't know."

Viviana was barely able to control her gasp of shock. "Talk to me."

Her heart was beating so fast as she listened to Lee reveal what had occurred between him and Angela that Viviana suddenly experienced lightheadedness.

"Have you thought about what she said?"

"Of course I have. It's either her way or we're through."

Leaning back, Viviana stared at her brother. The more she saw her father the more she saw the resemblance in the two men in voice intonation and body language. "Remember Aunt Babs telling us that Mama gave Daddy an ultimatum. That he get help with his drug problem or she was going to leave him. She died still loving and believing in him even though he loved his drugs more than he loved her. It's the same with you and Angela. You love the military more than you love her. Otherwise you would be able to understand her fear that she may lose another husband and father for her children. What are the odds of a woman standing at her husband's flag-draped coffin not once, but twice before she turns forty? Look at the number of guys from The Falls who come back after serving, settled into civilian life, started families and are living an uneventful life. Seth Collier gave the Corps twenty years and he's quite content serving as the sheriff of Wickham Falls."

"That's because he was military police, which means he made a lateral move to civilian law enforcement."

"Have you ever thought about what you would've done or been if you hadn't enlisted in the army?" The seconds ticked, becoming a full minute as Viviana waited for Lee's reply.

"The only thing I enjoy is cooking. I probably would've become a chef." Lee shook his head. "Why didn't I think of that when Angela talked about Sawyer, Aiden and Seth having a life after leaving the military?"

"Maybe it's because you were so hell-bent on returning to the Army that you didn't want to think of it. You're going to have to decide, Lee. The military or the woman you love. You can't have both, because Angela had both and you know how that ended. And it would be selfish on your part to put her through that again."

Lee closed his eyes. "What do I do, Vivi?"

"Go to Angela and let her know you love her too much to reenlist. That you're willing to talk about your options as a civilian."

Lee grabbed Viviana's shoulders and kissed her forehead. "Thanks, sis, for the pep talk. Now I have to go and see if we're still going to have a wedding next Saturday."

"We better!" she called out as he rushed out of the room.

The invitations had been mailed, and responses sent back by email. Viviana had ordered the food, flowers and decorations. And Angela had had her final fitting for her gown and she had also picked up Zoe's dress and Malcolm's outfit.

The wedding was scheduled exactly one week before the B and B's ribbon-cutting ceremony. Viviana closed her eyes and whispered a prayer that Lee would be able to convince Angela that he loved her enough to give up one dream to realize another.

The doorbell echoed throughout the house at the same time Angela finished reading *The Cat in the Hat* to Malcolm and Zoe. The Dr. Seuss titles were also their favorites because of the rhyming.

"You kids go upstairs and get into bed. I'll tuck you in as soon as I see who's at the door."

"Okay, Mama," they chimed in unison.

The first day Lee hadn't come to eat with them she made an excuse that he was busy and couldn't make it.

The second day the excuse was the same until Joyce gave her a look that said she knew something wasn't right. But it was Malcolm and Zoe who were clearly affected by his absence when they said no one could sit or touch his chair.

Angela peered through the security eye to see Lee standing on the porch. Her respiration increased as she opened the door and gasped. He had the same haunted look in his eyes as when he'd returned for Justin's funeral.

"May I come in?"

She inhaled a breath and stood aside for him enter. "Yes."

"Daddy!" Zoe screamed, making a beeline toward the door. He scooped her up in his arms and kissed her hair.

"Grammie, Daddy's here!" Malcolm yelled at the top of his tiny lungs.

Joyce emerged from her sewing room. Smiling, she pressed her palms together. "It's good seeing you again, Leland."

He shifted Zoe to one arm and cupped the back of Malcolm's head with his free hand. "Same here."

Malcolm patted his leg. "Are you coming up to tuck us in?"

"You do it better than Mama," Zoe said in a loud whisper.

Lee pressed his forehead to Zoe's. "That means I'm going to have to show Mama the way you like." Bending slightly, he set her down. "Go upstairs and get into bed and Daddy will be up as soon as I talk to Mama."

Angela bit back a smile. Lee was like the Pied Piper with her children. He was able to get the kids to do whatever he wanted without question, while it was *Why, Mama* whenever she asked them to do something.

She motioned to him with her head. "We'll talk on the porch."

"Are you coming for dinner tomorrow?" Joyce asked.

Lee stopped. "That all depends on your daughter-in-law."

Joyce glared at Angela. "Don't do or say something you might regret for the rest of your life. Yeah, I know I'm being a meddling mama-in-law, but my grandbabies love this man—"

"And I don't?" Angela countered angrily, cutting her off.

Joyce waved her hand in dismissal. "I give up. Forgive me for interfering."

Lee reached for Angela's hand. "Not to worry, Grammie. Everything is going to be okay."

"Do you really think everything is going to be okay because you say so?" she said accusingly when she and Lee stood on the porch.

"It will be after you hear what I have to say," Lee countered. "And Miss Joyce is right about her grandbabies loving me because I love them, too. I think I know what I'd like to do as a civilian."

Angela's mouth dropped. "Does this mean you're not going to reenlist?"

"Close your mouth, darling," Lee urged when he finished telling her about his plan to enroll in a culinary school and eventually take over as chef of the B and B.

"Where do you plan to go to culinary school?" Angela questioned.

"I'm thinking of applying to the same school where my Aunt Babs graduated."

"And where's that, Leland?"

"Charlotte, North Carolina."

"You're kidding, aren't you?"

Lee counted slowly to ten. He was willing to compromise and not reenlist, but even that didn't seem to please Angela. "No, I'm not, Angela. Do you really believe I'm going to marry you and leave you and our children behind?"

"Listen to yourself, Leland. If you re-up you still would leave us behind."

"This is different, babe. I plan to apply to Johnson and Wales University's Culinary Arts program. If I'm accepted, then I'd rent a house or an apartment for us. You've always talked about going to college, so the situation would be perfect for us."

"What about Malcolm and Zoe?"

He resisted the urge to roll his eyes. Lee didn't want to believe Angela was making it so difficult to agree to something that would prove beneficial to them both. He would use his GI educational benefits to pay for his tuition and there was a possibility that he could also secure housing at a reduced rate based on his military rank and number of years served.

"There are childcare facilities in North Carolina."

Angela rested her back against the porch column. She thought about everything Lee had proposed. And he was right about her wanting to attend and graduate college, but that would mean leaving The Falls until they completed their education. "It looks as if you've figured everything out."

"Not quite."

"What's missing, Lee?"

"You. Tell me now we're going to be married next Saturday or I'll walk away and never bother you again."

She bit her lip. She remembered him telling her the same thing when asking if he was competing with a dead man. Her chin trembled as she struggled not to cry. "I want you to bother me every day of my life we spend together."

"Is that a yes?"

Angela was so overcome with emotion that all she could do was nod. After she'd given Lee the ultimatum she thought she was being selfish, yet she knew there was no way she could go through losing another husband because he'd chosen to be a soldier.

"Yes, it's a yes."

She was given no time to react when Lee picked her up and kissed her in a passion that stole the breath from her lungs. She moaned when his hand searched under her blouse to cover her breast. Her hands were just as busy as she pulled up his tee and dug her fingers into the firm flesh covering his muscled back. It had been so long since they'd made love that she wanted to beg him to make love to her right there, but common sense prevailed.

The sounds from their labored breathing competed with the noise from emerging nocturnal wildlife. "Why don't you go upstairs and tuck your son and daughter in because it appears their mama just can't get it right," she teased.

"You don't have to get it right, Mama. There's one thing you can do that I'll never be able to do."

"What's that?"

Lee winked at her. "Grow a baby."

"Duh!" Angela's smile mirrored the happiness eddying through her and she turned and stared at the shadows in the encroaching dusk. Her life had come full circle. She never knew when she decided to befriend the new student sitting alone in the school's cafeteria that he would grow up to become her husband and father to her twins. She stayed on the porch until buzzing insects brushed against her exposed skin, and then went inside to break the news to Joyce that she was going to move to North Carolina for several years where she and Lee planned to attend college. Charlotte wasn't that far away and she was welcome to come and visit with her grandchildren anytime she wanted.

Chapter Thirteen

Angela held the bouquet of fall flowers in her left hand and rested her right on her father's as he led her down the white carpet on the grass under the enormous tent where the ceremony and reception would take place. The weather had cooperated with cool morning temperatures giving way to brilliant sunlight and seventy-degree readings.

Lee had declined having a military-style wedding because he did not want to be reminded of the weddings of his former buddies. Although he no longer thought of himself as a soldier he said he would always be an army ranger. He had selected Aiden Gibson as his best man.

Angela's gown was an unadorned sheath with narrow straps crisscrossing her bare back and a hint of a train. Her neatly braided shoulder-length hair was pinned on the nape of her long, slender neck with a jeweled hairclip. She'd attached a fingertip veil to the clip that had once belonged to Lee's great-grandmother. Viviana did double duty as maid of honor and assistant to the party planner.

Zoe and Malcolm, dressed in white, were adorable as flower girl and ring bearer, and when Nathan Banks escorted her past the rows with her mother and Joyce, Angela noticed they were dabbing their eyes.

She had insisted on an informal celebration sans tuxedos and ties, and with comfortable shoes for the women. Only Lee and Aiden wore neckwear for the ceremony and the photos to follow, and both joked they didn't like wearing legal nooses.

When the pastor asked who was giving this woman in marriage Nathan Banks's deep voice reverberated throughout the tent, eliciting laughs and giggles from the assembly. Angela could not bring her gaze away from Lee as she mouthed the appropriate responses. Pinpoints of heat stung her cheeks when she saw desire lurking in the depths of the blue-gray eyes making love to her.

He untied the ribbon on the pillow holding the rings and smiled at Malcolm. "Thank you, son." Lee repeated his vows as he slipped the platinum band on Angela's finger.

Angela repeated the action when she slipped a matching band on Lee's hand. Less than a minute later the pastor pronounced them man and wife. And when she felt Lee's mouth touch hers she knew Justin was smiling down on her and his best friend.

They turned to face the assembly amid applause and whistling. She shared a tender smile with Lee when he raised her left hand and kissed her fingers. "I love you," she mouthed as he nodded in acknowledgment.

Flashes from cameras and phones went off as those

in attendance captured the joy in the newlyweds' eyes as they continued to stare lovingly at each other. Angela stopped long enough to hug her father-in-law. "Thank you for your son," she whispered in his ear.

Emory smiled. "He'll be a good father and husband."

"I know he will."

She and Lee stood in a receiving line to greet and thank their guests for sharing their special day, and she knew the next time she and Lee celebrated it would be to welcome the birth of their third child.

* * * * *

MILLS & BOON

Coming next month

SURPRISE BABY FOR THE HEIR
Ellie Darkins

'I'm pregnant.'

The words hit Fraser like a bus, rendering him mute and paralysed. He sat in silence for long, still moments, letting the words reverberate through his ears, his brain. The full meaning of them fell upon him slowly, gradually. Like being crushed to death under a pile of small rocks. Each one so insignificant that you didn't feel the difference, but collectively, they stole his breath, and could break his body.

'Are you going to say anything?' Elspeth asked, breaking into his thoughts at last. He met her gaze and saw that it had hardened even further – he hadn't thought that that would be possible. And he could understand why. He'd barely said a word since she'd dropped her bombshell. But he needed time to take this in. Surely she could understand that. 'I'm sorry. I'm in shock,' he said. Following it up with the first thing that popped into his head. 'We were careful.'

'Not careful enough, it seems.' Her voice was like ice, cutting into him, and he knew that it was the wrong thing to say. He wasn't telling her anything she didn't know.

Fraser shook his head.

'What do you want to do?' he asked, his voice tentative,

aware that they had options. Equally aware that discussing them could be a minefield if they weren't on the same page.

'I want to have the baby,' Elspeth said with the same firmness and lack of equivocation that she had told him that she was pregnant. How someone so slight could sound so immovably solid was beyond him, and a huge part of her appeal, he realised. Something that he should be wary of…

Continue reading
SURPRISE BABY FOR THE HEIR
Ellie Darkins

Available next month
www.millsandboon.co.uk

COMING SOON!

We really hope you enjoyed reading this book. If you're looking for more romance, be sure to head to the shops when new books are available on

Thursday 24th January

To see which titles are coming soon, please visit

millsandboon.co.uk/nextmonth

LET'S TALK
Romance

For exclusive extracts, competitions
and special offers, find us online:

facebook.com/millsandboon

@MillsandBoon

@MillsandBoonUK

Get in touch on 01413 063232

For all the latest titles coming soon, visit
millsandboon.co.uk/nextmonth